The Potato Eaters

STORIES

Farhad Pirbal

Translated from the Kurdish by
Jiyar Homer and Alana Marie Levinson-LaBrosse

DEEP VELLUM PUBLISHING
DALLAS, TEXAS

Deep Vellum Publishing
3000 Commerce St., Dallas, Texas 75226
deepvellum.org · @deepvellum

Deep Vellum is a 501c3 nonprofit literary arts organization
founded in 2013 with the mission to bring
the world into conversation through literature.

Copyright © 2000 by Farhad Pirbal
Translation copyright © 2024 by Jiyar Homer and Alana Marie Levinson-LaBrosse
Originally published as مالی شەرەفخانی بەتلیسی by پەنتاتەخۆرەمکان (Sharafkhan Bidlisi
Publishing House, Hawler, Kurdistan, 2000).

FIRST ENGLISH EDITION, 2024

Support for this publication has been provided in part by the National Endowment for the
Arts, the Texas Commission on the Arts, the City of Dallas Office of Arts and Culture, the
Communities Foundation of Texas, and the Addy Foundation.

LIBRARY OF CONGRESS CATALOGING-IN-PUBLICATION DATA

Names: Pîrbal, Ferhad, 1961- author. | Homer, Jiyar, translator. |
Levinson-LaBrosse, Alana Marie, translator. | Khakpour, Porochista,
writer of introduction.
Title: The potato eaters : stories / Farhad Pirbal ; translated from the
Kurdish by Jiyar Homer and Alana Marie Levinson-LaBrosse.
Other titles: Petatexorekan. English
Description: First edition. | Dallas, Texas : Deep Vellum Publishing, 2024.
Identifiers: LCCN 2024007208 (print) | LCCN 2024007209 (ebook) | ISBN
9781646052707 (trade paperback) | ISBN 9781646052912 (ebook)
Subjects: LCSH: Pîrbal, Ferhad, 1961---Translations into English. | LCGFT:
Short stories.
Classification: LCC PK6908.9.P568 P4813 2024 (print) | LCC PK6908.9.P568
(ebook) | DDC 891/.5973--dc23/eng/20240403
LC record available at https://lccn.loc.gov/2024007208
LC ebook record available at https://lccn.loc.gov/2024007209
ISBN (TPB) 978-1-64605-270-7 | ISBN (Ebook) 978-1-64605-291-2

Cover design by Pablo Marin, Verbum.Media

Interior layout and typesetting by KGT

PRINTED IN THE UNITED STATES OF AMERICA

CONTENTS

"We Are the Sacrifice of Our Time": On Farhad Pirbal's *The Potato Eaters*

An Introduction by Porochista Khakpour

Farhad Pirbal entered my life at the worst time possible, which really could not have been more perfect. I had more on my plate than ever, and that should not be read in the glamorously dismissive way some literary elite refer to their projects. I was too busy, of course, but not because of the muses. I was late on my tax extension; my elderly dog was not thriving; my partner and I were at each other's throats. Also, our four-hundred-something-square-foot studio apartment had become a nonstop construction zone—a galling symphony of drills and hammers and saws was our daily soundtrack, results of demolition and renovation of the scale you recognize just might be there to con old tenants out so they can quadruple rents. *Broke, tired, sick* was my daily anti-affirmation. All was bad.

Maybe because I'd heard of him or because I have an interest in Kurdish writers or because Deep Vellum does great books, something told me to say yes to writing this introduction amidst the chaos. In came the manuscript and I continued to fall apart, but by the time I got lost in these stories, the world was falling apart with me. Suddenly our world was back in wartime, the kind of war we never quite witness—not like this at least, a hell of baby limbs and blood and guts and debris and missile whistles and mothers' screams and the never-ending toxic discourse of too-comfortable, theory-poisoned scholars and analysts, an inevitability broadcast from every last-gasping social media platform. *Broke, tired, sick*, said the world back to us. Then we moved into a new apartment that sounded too good to be true and then *was* too good to be true; instead of construction sounds all day every day, there were low-flying airplanes ascending from and descending to a local airport at such low altitude that they evoked fighter jets deploying for combat. My first memories on this planet happen to be the first years of the Iran-Iraq War and so anything approaching the theatrics of armed conflict easily blisters into all-too-familiar panic for me. This was my origin story as a refugee, after all. *Broke, tired, sick*. I began to dream of leaving this place, any place; I began feeling like I was truly losing my mind a little, and instead of friends consoling me when they heard that, their answer became, "Yes, me too."

At my preferred hours to read and write, the night owl's nine–five, I started reading and reading. In a way, all my despairs, old and new, found a perfect home in the Pirbalian universe.

How does one describe Farhad Pirbal to Western readers? Could he be a bit Charles Bukowski? Maybe a bit Gregory Corso, Oscar Zeta Acosta, Hunter S. Thompson, William Gay—plus a touch of the surrealists and Dadaists from Europe, and don't forget a dash of the mischievous Sufi agitators of the East! But the truth is, trying to find someone to compare Pirbal to is useless, as he is that rare, near-mythic true original. We are all destined to be bad imitators of his if we're lucky! But his singularity goes further than just words on a page. After all, what literary tradition can boast a prolific genius of this magnitude who also spends his spare time going in and out of prison for everything from disorderly conduct to arson. (I promise I'll get to that.) You—probably broke, tired, and sick as I am (and Pirbal is too!)—know it would be as useless to blame the poet as it would to blame poetry. Especially in this case: for as much as Pirbal seems to struggle with the world he's in, I can't help but feel it's the world that's somehow fallen short of him.

—

Farhad Pirbal is a sixty-two-year-old writer, philosopher, singer, poet, painter, and critic from Hawler, Southern Kurdistan. As translator, scholar, and my friend Shook wrote in a beautiful essay on him for *Poetry Foundation*, Pirbal "may be the greatest innovator of Kurdish literature in the twentieth century, in both poetry and prose."

I'd just add that it goes further than great: Pirbal is one of the most unforgettable icons of the Kurdish art world—the kind of public figure who gets stopped on the street—and for good reason. He is a social media fiend, extremely present on Instagram, TikTok, Facebook, Twitter. There's something absolutely charming about this kind of extremely accessible anti-celebrity; against your will you'll find yourself mesmerized by his wild-eyed, shaggy-haired, ever-gesticulating presence, demanding you hear him. He's not easy to forget. He looks like the kind of guy who is not quite an old man, but who has looked like one his whole life, his signature overgrown mustache giving off eccentricity and affability. He was a renowned mad professor and he looks like it, the sort of West Asian genius whose earthy crudeness tempers a slightly mystical air. Everything about him is equal parts intimidating and lovable.

All you have to do is search his name on Twitter to see all kinds of hero worship from a young audience. Some of it is due to his attention to human rights activism—Pirbal has not been shy about pushing back against ruling parties and politicians of all kinds. But the rest seems to be due to mostly, well, vibes. "babe wake up! Farhad Pirbal is having another meltdown!" an account in Hawler quips; "I have activated my farhad pirbal mode and life is getting better," a young Kurdish woman in traditional Newroz garb declares; there's even a tweet which features a very bizarre, ornate portrait of him and Adele set to a thrillingly addictive mash-up of her song "Set Fire to the Rain" with Pirbal's tumultuous oratory.

The kids aren't just making fun. They know this is a scholar, that he studied Kurdish language and literature at the University of Salahadin. They know that in 1986, he left Kurdistan for France, where he continued his Kurdish literature studies at the Sorbonne. They know about the cultural center he set up in the mid '90s in Southern Kurdistan. They know this man deserves the highest level of respect.

But they also know everything else, and that's the line where the normal stuff ends. You can't talk Pirbal without getting into his infamy.

Pirbal has not been shy about talking about all this

and neither has his family. A few years ago, his family turned to the public, urging for his arrest as a step towards rehabilitation:

> We, the family of Dr. Farhad, are very saddened by his inappropriate and unfair behavior in the Kurdistan Region's cities and towns, especially in the city of Hawler, and especially by his verbal attacks and foul language against public figures and officials. We seek an apology from all the parties. He is suffering from psychological problems and is addicted to drugs. His health conditions are very bad . . . He is currently a threat to the safety and security of the public. Hence, we call on the KRG to take quick and appropriate measures against him . . .

But in July 2019, things took a turn for the worse. Pirbal went as far as setting the Wafaiy House library on fire, videotaping his arson and posting it on Facebook. Rumors have swirled that he was upset about copyright infringement and not getting paid on time, but he was arrested within hours and spent some months in prison again. The charges were ultimately dropped, as was a lawsuit.

Pirbal, the mischievous trouble-making trickster who

seems to get away with everything, is a little irresistible in our chaotic times (or entertaining at least!). But there's also another way his penchant for self-sabotage hits home: Pirbal is the most uncompromising survivor in letters. And at least for those of us of the *broke, tired, sick* ilk, we need this story too.

—

In my literary circles, everyone loves to relay the endearing anecdote of Kafka laughing uncontrollably while reading some of his darkest writing to friends. You can find Pirbal in that anecdote too, but take his essence dipped in acid and processed through a blender. There's laughter, sure, but there's something else, perhaps some singing then scream-ing then crying then laughing again, then the kind of crying that becomes laughter that becomes crying that becomes laughter . . . the uproar only certain men equally exalted and fallen seem made of.

Some of us will just get it, for others it might take a sec-ond. But for me reading Pirbal felt like therapy—just like hearing about his life somehow felt healing. There are few truly outlandish iconoclasts left, it feels like, and if they exist the mainstream certainly hasn't let them become a celebrity the way Pirbal has. Pirbal is for the overeducated who have given up their concept of those laurels; he's for the extremely prolific writers who constantly threaten to never write again; he's for the messy artists who make everyone a bit nervous with their insistence on messes; he's gonna wreck someone's night but you hope it's not yours so you can just watch. He's the miracle of second, third, fourth, fifth, sixth, etc. chances for the bad kids—and there's nothing consoling about his life. There is no happy ending in his own story or his own stories. Maybe the only happy ending is evidence of him so defiantly alive on the page, on the streets, on the internet.

—

Is it possible to put Pirbal the man aside for a moment and just marvel at the stories in *The Potato Eaters*? I was delighted to realize, yes, the creation more than lives up to the saga of the creator.

To begin with, these stories are a master class in all kinds of formal innovation. His prose is the work of a poet. He utilizes syntactical precision and structural economy with the same intensity with which he sets free entire passages into the lush and unapologetically orchestral wild. Metaphors pierce reality and the figurative turns literal without warning.

Footnotes work like you've never seen them work before. The second person is employed so masterfully you barely notice the shift. The absurdist plot points melt into earnest interludes of longing and despair, then just as quickly dance over to defiance and exuberance, before landing back at absurdism. Timing is everything with Pirbal: there is a calculus to his measured revolutions into mayhem. Repetition gives the work a lyrical quality at times; at others, the almost maddening cut-and-pastes dare you to be a lazy, skimming reader. But as with all things Pirbal, you know you'd be missing too much, so there's only reading and rereading here.

The themes will never leave you. Whether Pirbal's characters are in Copenhagen or Paris or a small Kurdish village, home is not ever a simple proposition. There's displacement, refugee life, exile, desertion and abandonment, loneliness and solitude, the feeling of never belonging, the isolation of the artist. Some Americans may fall into the trap of seeing these all as simply expressions of Kurdish statelessness, but Pirbal lets his allegories hover in the ether of profound universality. Pirbal is performing his truth, which is often his people's truth, but it may not be much of an accident when you find yourself pacing in and out of his sets too.

In one of my favorite pieces, the parable "The Deserter," a soldier has left his right leg back at the base and goes looking for it. As you'd expect, the misadventures are count-less, but the piece ends up in a letter to his leg, with these lines that made me tear up: "My generation and I—desper-ate, ill-fated youth—we are the sacrifice of our time, the sac-rifice that these idiots and asses we call leaders today make to the filthy gods of war. I'm just so tired, so very, very tired."

Two stories later, Pirbal burns clauses and sentences and entire paragraphs to dissect the dilemma of so many dis-placed peoples. In "A Refugee," Pirbal renders repetition in modes slapstick to hypnotic, the horrible dark comedy of this sequence appearing thirteen times:

> The refugee, consumed by desire, ate the first banana and threw the peel onto the sidewalk, ate the second banana and threw the peel onto the sidewalk, ate the third banana and threw the peel onto the sidewalk, ate the fourth banana and threw the peel onto the side-walk, ate the fifth banana and threw the peel onto the sidewalk, ate the sixth banana and threw the peel onto the sidewalk, ate the seventh banana and threw the peel onto the sidewalk, ate the eighth banana and threw the peel onto the sidewalk, ate the ninth banana and threw the peel onto the sidewalk, ate the tenth banana and threw the peel onto the sidewalk.

Even when you know Pirbal is playing a game with you—
against you?—it's impossible to resist him. I never skimmed,
just reread and reread. In the title story—possibly my
favorite, but every piece was my favorite at some point—
we learn of a village that has become obsessed with making the most of potatoes, from potato arak to potato soap.
When Fereydun visits his family and brings them gold, they
are baffled:

His cousin, from his mother's brother, said, "Well,
that's strange! Why didn't you bring any potatoes
from abroad?"

Fereydun, calmly: "Why is that strange? I didn't
bring any potatoes from abroad."

Fereydun's father, at last, with sorrow and grief,
took a tragic, desperate breath: "Well, but why, my
son? Why didn't you bring any potatoes with you?"

Fereydun, mustering his pride at the thought of
the great value of the gold, said, "I brought only gold
with me."

His maternal uncle, a dark-skinned, broad-
shouldered man with a sweeping handlebar mustache, with curiosity, wondered aloud, "What is gold,
my boy?"

You get the feeling Pirbal can't help himself with stylis-
tic hijinks delivered in a very darkly comic register—after
all, experimental machinations paired with deeply serious
themes are his comfort zone. It's hard not to fall in love with
the format of "Schizophrenia," an exploration of alternate
endings and plot point swapping a la Choose Your Own
Adventure or Julio Cortázar's *Hopscotch*. And there's a very
poignant eight-word story—a poem really, three lines, with
the white space of the page allowing those eight words to
cascade next to their ellipses with an almost startling fluid-
ity—which gets the title "An epic tragic story." (I won't say
much more lest I spoil the eight words!)

And then there are these other times when you really
hear Pirbal as if he's looking you straight in the eye and
confessing everything—those sequences moved and
chilled me the most. Pirbalian confrontation has a power
you can't get over easily. I can't tell you how many times I
found myself rereading this passage in "A New Address" at
various 3:00 AMs:

> You light a cigarette. This isn't your first time. You
> remember how many other times you ran from your
> cramped and crowded house, from your stunned
> mother and wasted father, the father you couldn't

seem to accept as your father no matter how hard you tried. He constantly spat at you, cursing, raising a fist or a belt, driving you like a stray into the neighborhood's cold, dark alleys. The only peace and comfort in your life was in those moments when the night reached out to stroke your hair with her fingers, when your father, under cover of that darkness, with a few other mustachioed, muscle-bound men, walked over to the nearby café to gamble and drink. You know that man, that king of cowards who hates books. The man who tears up and burns every book you buy and read. The kind of man who makes you love time more than luck. But here it is: This evening, once and for all, you left. You picked yourself up and left, without looking back.

Thanks to magnificent translators Jiyan Homer and Alana Marie Levinson-LaBrosse, a whole new world can now feel the power of those sentences. Very few of Farhad Pirbal's forty-three books have been translated into English, but with this volume I hope the world demands to read more. I know I will. There are few writers, I think, who can address this—or any!—terrifying moment in history with the wit, depth, brilliance, and sense of legacy Pirbal has. It reminds me of a couple sentences from "The Desert" that I would have highlighted in blood if I could: "The terrible, empty silence of the place enveloped me. I felt fatally alone and foreign." Being in Pirbal's company these past months was a break from that exact sensation. I envy anyone who is about to turn these pages for the first time. As the world around us keeps insisting on ending in new and more horrible ways with each era—how to unhear the phantom fighter jets at my window! how to un-scroll and unsee someone's baby's clenched fist without a body! how to untangle a strand of justice out of every politician's bale of burnt verbiage!—the poet's voice that can sing and scream, laugh and cry, whisper and roar—especially all at once—is not just gravely needed but maybe really and truly all that's left for us to hear.

Porochista Khakpour

New York City, November 2023

The Margins of Europe

AT FOUR THIRTY IN THE MORNING, I got myself up, stuffed some things in a backpack, and went to Nørreport Station.[1] I bought a round-trip ticket and immediately boarded the train to Skagen, nearly twenty-eight hours from Copenhagen.

Sixteen or more hours passed as I ate, relieved myself, washed my face, and walked around. All the while I thought, Should I go or not? Should I go or not? Finally, I decided, I'm going. I will be the young monk delivering medicine to heal his mother's blind eyes.

Why not? I imagined my trip's intention as its most defining feature. Knocking on her door would usher in a

---

1. A Copenhagen train station. Trains bound for Denmark's northern islands depart there.

paradise, end a tragedy, rescue the fate and life of one person, even two.[2]

"Thank you." Kurdo said, as he accepted a cigarette from his seatmate, an old woman.

"Are you a painter, sir?" she asked.

"No."

"Still . . . that's so beautiful . . . may I have a look? What are these elegant lines and images in your notebook?"

Kurdo didn't understand all the spoken Danish. "May we speak English?"

"Yes, of course. Ah, do you not know Danish well?

---

2. Once, eighteen years ago, Kurdo, my story's protagonist, in his homeland, in Khanaqin, had read a Russian novel which told of a young nobleman who tossed and turned in his bed, racked by isolation and solitude. The lonely young man didn't know how to help his loneliness or escape from his hell: his seclusion and solitude. A close friend had admonished the character, "My friend, find something that interests you or find someone to love!" So Kurdo found himself in his seat, on the train, with only an old Danish woman sitting opposite him, thinking back on that Russian novel. He thought and turned the pages of a small, red notebook, occasionally writing notes for his memoirs.

The old Danish woman was obviously looking over Kurdo's shoulder at the small, red notebook in his hands. She was curious and wanted to get Kurdo, the strange refugee, to talk. In the end, the old Danish woman, against all Danish traditions, offered Kurdo a cigarette to start a conversation.

Excuse me, sir. I asked you what these beautiful images are in this notebook."

"These are not images, but writing, Kurdish writing in Arabic script."

"I'm overcome. I'm sorry. I can't help laughing as if my heart's been thrown open by these beautiful lines, this calligraphy, these images you call script. Your writing is so magical and deeply artistic; it possesses a majesty our script doesn't. How many years have you lived here as a refugee?"

"One year and eight months."

"Where do you live?"

"Copenhagen. Are you a painter, ma'am?"

"Me? I just draw for fun. That's why these stunning lines of writing in your notebook caught my attention. So, you're a Kurd!"

"Yes. Nice to meet you, ma'am. My name is Kurdo."

"Birgitte. I've only read news of your people in the papers."

"Sorry, ma'am, your name was . . .?"

"Birgitte."[3]

---

3. Kurdo, when he heard the name "Birgitte," fell silent for a while. Later, almost unconscious of the old woman's existence, he murmured, from the bottom of his heart, "It is a beautiful name."

The old woman, clearly enjoying that Kurdo had said so, replied, "That's kind of you."

"And what do you draw, ma'am?"

"Solitude! Solitude is my only subject. You like the visual arts?"

"Many of my friends were painters. I've lived with them. So my heart, too, is deeply moved by the visual arts. I often look through books and albums only for the images."

"I've spent more than half my life drawing. See my yellowed fingers? Drawing so much made them mutiny with wrinkles and creases; even my eyes, my eyes are nearly gone from drawing."

The old woman laughed then and, with a child's earthiness and innocence, raised her glasses to her eyes, "See, my dear sir?"

"You must have had many shows."

"Never. I never even asked a gallery to consider my work. I just draw for fun."[4]

"Do you know Keerkgard?" Kurdo asked.

"Who?"

Her silence, which had been somewhere between shyness and repression, became speechlessness as she looked out the window.

4. Kurdo felt tragic beauty, knowledge, and humanity just under the skin of this sixty-five-year-old woman, behind every word she said. Especially when she spoke of solitude, saying, "Solitude! Solitude is my only subject." That's what suddenly brought Kierkegaard to mind.

"Keerkgard!"

"Oh . . . Kierkegaard! I adore him. How do you know him?"

"I have read a few texts about him."

"Ah, now I see why all of the sudden you thought of Kierkegaard. My life, art, and fate are utterly like his. Kierkegaard and I are absolutely, through to our marrow, Danish, and Denmark is this: solitude, solitude, solitude. That's precisely why I said, 'Solitude is my only subject.'"

So, in the train car, Kurdo completely forgot himself and everything to do with his trip, even its intent. Curious, eager, he fell into the fascinating issues and complexities of the old woman's life; particularly because it was the first time in his life he had had such conversation with a Dane, he hoped to drag the conversation out, "It's true, I've only lived a year and eight months in Denmark, but today's Denmark doesn't strike me as the Denmark of Kierkegaard's age."

"What you see now is the outermost form and face. You haven't yet reached the root, the dregs of it. All Danish people, always, every second, feel lonely and afraid: fearful under threat of separation, fragmentation, isolation. This and: Setting aside those who are just lonely themselves or live alone, have you read about the suicide rates attributed to loneliness? The newspapers say that Sweden's suicide rate surpasses that of every other European country. But our country's statistics remain alarming to me. Whatever the comparison, this loneliness belongs to all of Europe, not just Sweden and Denmark, though the tragedy of solitude seems particularly palpable to me in Denmark. As well, though, we are a small nation, all of us together total only five million people, you know, and one million of that five are refugees."

"I didn't know Danish people felt loneliness so keenly."

"Indeed we do. We Danes, even all of Europe, as I said, we run from this loneliness, we form groups—out of fear of loneliness, we take leaps of faith in one another and rush into marriage, or for a sense of adventure head out to Africa and Asia, but especially the East. I think it's even possible to say: He who feels no loneliness is no Dane, no European, here where loneliness permeates every inch of human life."

At that moment, Kurdo remembered a poem of Rimbaud's, "Bad Blood," and said to himself, "That's right." He asked the old lady painter, "But this reality must permeate each artist's perspective?"

"I would say, as I understand it: A Danish artist, if he doesn't speak of the loneliness and solitude of Danish people, is no Dane and perhaps even has lost touch with the pulse of the solitary heart of Europe. An artist must sound the alarm and bring our awareness to our own tragedy. Kierkegaard, a hundred fifty years ago, predicted that today this would be the general state of Danish and European people: to writhe within the pain of loneliness."

Then, the old woman, as if she had poured out whatever sorrow and heartbreak she carried, sighed with relief. She lit another cigarette, opened her flowered purse, took out a little makeup kit, and lifted a small mirror in her hands to see her face.

Kurdo took the opportunity to examine the wrinkles and creases of her cheeks, which grew out over the ruins of an old, luscious beauty, and also to notice, for the first time, that dentures made the rows of her lower teeth. It was remarkable that all this lustrous old woman's aging, after almost sixty-five years, hadn't ground down her humanity, her soul or inner beauty.

Kurdo didn't want her to sense his thoughts, these observations, and yet did want to ask, "Ma'am, I'm sorry, but how old are you?"

But he knew this was not a pretty question, or a cultured thing. If he focused too much on the red blotches running down her neck and her two great, weeping breasts, both engulfed by signs of miserable old age, perhaps the simmering heat and obsessive intensity she felt behind their conversation would die down. So, he didn't ask if she was a widow or divorced, if she had children or not, if she was wealthy or just comfortable. In his gut, he knew, 'All these questions are meaningless if the person I'm asking feels lonely. The old woman feels she has no one, that she is rotting in solitude. That's it. That's the only concern.'

"I myself am alone. And I feel my loneliness keenly," the old woman said suddenly, under her breath. Then, looking through the train car's windows toward the distant, escaping mountains, she said, "You Eastern people are different. The East is another thing altogether."

Kurdo had no desire to confess anything important about himself, but to comfort this solitary, supple-souled old woman, he said, "Since I came to Denmark, I have felt that for every one of the twenty-seven years of my life I have lived in solitude."

Kurdo wanted to speak more honestly and say, "Since I came to Denmark, I haven't been able to get close to a Danish woman, come to know her, breathe in the scent of her neck." But he thought this confession would make him seem weak.

"So, you do see? But before you were comforting me?"

"Ma'am, I'm a refugee. I don't know your language, your

culture, your customs . . . I have no work here. A refugee like me, it's my last remaining right to live alone, remain alone, feel alone."

"I'll talk about your country: In your country, you are for each other, with each other! I don't know. From Orientalist books, movies, and anecdotes, I understood that you Easterners don't know what loneliness and separation are, but that you live as an example of love and cohesion and coexistence and family and unity."

"But I'm sure you see—it must be obvious to you that all us Easterners yearn for Europe."

"Because you're running from the clutches of a war imposed on you."

"No. Because we want the progress of Europe."

"So, then, want a different Europe, make a different Europe for yourselves!"

"Why? Why different?"

"Because our Europe, today's Europe, is loneliness, a fatal loneliness! We created our Europe for ourselves. You must be brave and create your own Europe!"[5]

---

5. Kurdo was a little offended. He felt she had called out his weakness. What did she mean, "We created our Europe for ourselves. You must be brave and create your own Europe!"? Did she mean, "You Kurds in your country are sluggish and stupid, absorbed only in fighting and chaining up your women and girls just so you can

Kurdo's eyes broke. The old woman's words weighed heavily on him and he broke once more. But he didn't want to seem broken or defeated before this clever, straight-talking old woman, so he tried to speak as bluntly as she had, "Here I have no woman and no home, but I have never felt loneliness to be fatal."

"I only meant to say: You, if your situation were unchanged except that you remained in your country, would you feel content?"

"Yes. But I couldn't stay in my country."

"Sure, I know, there is war, but my question is about systems: family, social, and spiritual."

---

escape to Europe to seek out sex, women, wisdom, and comfort?" Or did she mean to tell Kurdo, "Here you are, with the same conclusions that caused you to leave your country. And you thought Europe was heaven on earth." But of course this old woman, this old painter, had met many refugees like him in Denmark and knew every secret of the lone refugee! Being from this country, how could she be so dense? How could she not know the situation a Kurdish man and refugee faces in Denmark? How his life is and isn't? Maybe at this exact moment, she was pitying Kurdo's situation and understanding fully how deadening and perverse life can be for a refugee—from Lebanon, Palestine, Sri Lanka, India, anywhere—for a man of twenty-seven, to be without a woman.

The pain and reversals and grief of all those long, late nights, when you leave a pulsating nightclub or a bar packed with women, drunk and alone and empty-handed without a girl, a woman, or even a widow to wish you goodnight as you turn out the light!

"Of course. I'm with you."

"I miss my ex-husband, my children, I miss my childhood, my teenage years, my young adulthood. Europe misses its sixteenth and seventeenth and eighteenth and nineteenth centuries . . . "

"As I miss my city."

"So we are, all of us, strangers, alone. Each of us miss something, someone, each of us lacking something, someone . . . we need one another . . . we want one another . . . and still, we are wretched."[6]

At this, the two fell together into a distant, sorrowful silence; softly, without shedding a tear, they wept over the corpses of their loneliness and solitude.

Just then, Kurdo noticed the old woman's tired face: Her heavy eyelids, behind her square-framed glasses, were closing, little by little. She was falling asleep. Perhaps it had been quite some time since she had spoken so much. Kurdo, too, had rarely spoken so much as he had today, even with his Kurdish friends in Copenhagen or the other refugees in his apartment building from Iran, Lebanon, Sri Lanka, and Palestine. He, too, was tired. So very tired.

---

6. Kurdo murmured to himself, "I didn't know Europe would so humiliate me, alone, having no one. And I had no idea Europe itself was so sorrowful, lonely, and fraught."

Kurdo leaned his head back into the tender chair and fell to imagining his lover: Immediately he remembered the morning when the postman stood on the far side of the door, knock, knock, knocking, and shoved a bundle of newspapers, advertisements, and leaflets through the mail slot, into the room. To dispel the boredom and loneliness, he flipped through the paper, page by page, until in a corner, under "Personals," he saw a beautiful, young, blonde-haired, blue-eyed girl. Under the photograph, she had written that she was from Skagen city, living on Jylland Island in northern Denmark, in Taastrup Alley, Brøndby Street, House No. 7. She wanted to meet a handsome, hot-blooded Eastern man but had two conditions: (1) he must be a refugee with a residency card, speaking either Danish or English well, and (2) he must love literature, painting, and reading and be a romantic, passionate man!

So, he, Kurdo, Kurdo of the chevron mustache, Kurdo the hot-blooded and handsome, Kurdo whose looks and style had, in years gone by, been the talk of beautiful girls first throughout Khanaqin's Thawra High School, then the University of Mosul's English Department and College of Literature, he who had, for nearly two years, not tasted a woman or inhaled the scent of a girl's neck (that's right, here, in Europe, you can't get a girl even with looks and style!), he sank so deep into loneliness and celibacy and solitude, he buried his manhood in the slit of his folded-up mattress. His friends Saman, Abdulla, Maghdid, Zhilwan, all lived with older women—fifty, sixty years old—but he couldn't manage even that.

To be fair, twice he'd had a chance to do something like that: once in an Irish bar and another time in Tivoli, but he hadn't really wanted to, couldn't fully want to—he felt ashamed—as if people were pointing fingers at him. Isn't it good that unlike Sherwan and Rahim he didn't go shack up with a hermaphrodite or do it with some man who wanted to become a woman? So, why not? Why not try out this path, through this gate? It was a trip and a respite, barreling forward in a train car. He dreamed, he had desire, so why not? Why not go? A beautiful, trim Danish girl—so, she had her demands: a romantic, passionate man who loves literature and painting and reading. That must mean she is the same kind of girl who loves the same kind of things. Perhaps in Europe girls who live outside the capital, in far-flung cities or villages, don't share the same nature and norms as girls in the capital or big cities. They aren't so haughty. They don't look down their noses. They retain their lowland simplicity and girlishness.

Yes, they aren't completely defiled by the hands of

overcrowded, selfish European civilization. Maybe girls outside the city, in villages, run with the same sweet, girl-ish blood our girls do. But why hadn't he shaved his giant chevron mustache clean off at home before he got on the train? Danish girls, in general, don't like mustaches. So, a lit-tle later, in the train restroom, he decided he'd shave.

But no, no, what makes him himself? What has made him himself? He'll stay just so. Who's to say? Maybe she'll be one of those girls who likes mustaches. Let it be what it will be![7]

"The moment the train left Copenhagen's Sjælland Island for Odense Island, it entered a colossal ship. The ship then con-ducted the train into the city of Odense on the sea's back. Right then, I didn't have the heart to wake you. You were sleeping—such a deep sleep—so I stepped outside alone to have breakfast on the deck."

Kurdo replied, "I didn't know that would happen. When I woke up, the train had stopped, and it seemed the train had gone into the belly of a ship. The whole world had gone dark. And you had fallen asleep. A passenger—an old man—had

---

7. Kurdo, opposite the old woman, little by little, his eyelids meet-ing each other, fell asleep; he arrived in Skagen dreaming these sweet dreams.

sat down next to you. I got up, went to the bathroom, ate, and came back."

"Yes, to make the crossing between Odense and Sjælland Islands, the train boarded a second ship."

"This is the first time I have traveled this way."

"So, where are you going?"

"Skagen."

"Really?"

"Yes."

"That's where I'm from."

"Did work take you to Copenhagen?"

"No. For over twenty-two years, I haven't gone to Copenhagen. From the moment my husband and I separated, I haven't left Skagen. This was my first trip back to Copenhagen in twenty-two years. I went to visit my son; I haven't seen him for more than three years."

Kurdo, looking at the old woman and listening, suddenly—though he himself didn't know why—felt how very heavy the old woman's face was; he felt it suddenly heavy on his heart: this distant destination, this long haul with this prattling, dried-up old hound of a woman.

"How much longer until we reach Skagen?" he asked.

"We passed Aalborg some time ago." She looked at her watch. "I would think we'll get there in about fifteen minutes." At this, the old woman got to her feet and moved toward the train car door. "I'll just run to the restroom."[8]

The train came to a stop, and the old woman picked up her purse and shouldered her backpack; Kurdo had only his backpack, which he settled on his shoulders. With the crowd from the train, they stepped onto the platform at Skagen Station. It was about eight AM.

When they stepped out onto the city streets, Kurdo lifted his eyes to the bright mountains, far away, on the edge of town, and said, "Skagen is a beautiful city."

"But it seems small. Doesn't it?"

"Compared to Copenhagen, yes."

"Skagen is the last city in northern Denmark. Here, we share a border with Norway. The other side of that mountain is Norway! So, will you tell me: Why have you come to the edge of the world?"

Kurdo still hadn't told the old woman of that day when in a newspaper's advertisement pages, in the corner of a

---

8. The old woman, when she came back, quickly grabbed her bags from overhead and told Kurdo:

   "Get ready! We're here."

   "Skagen?!"

   "Yes, yes. Come on. Gather your things! And tell me, would you like me to show you around my city?"

   "Yes. If it's no bother and you have the time."

   "It would be my pleasure. You're a stranger here."

personals page, he saw a beautiful, young, blonde-haired, blue-eyed girl who, under her photograph, had written she was from Skagen, living in Taastrup Alley, Brøndby Street, House No. 7, and wanted to meet a handsome, hot-blooded Eastern man, and . . . now, he had come to find that beautiful, young girl.

No, he hadn't told her, he felt ashamed by it, or at least felt this (especially if the old woman were to see) as a lack in his character. Whatever the case, he thought, it's not necessary to confess this. So he said, "I've come to visit a friend of mine."

"In which neighborhood?"

"Taastrup."

"Really?"

"Yes."

"That's my neighborhood. And look, the bus has arrived."

The bus, riding the city's spine, had gone about fifteen minutes from the city center. Among thousands of trees and green foothills were a few houses sunk in the morning's gentle haze. Taking in all this natural beauty, I had nothing to say, no questions for her.

The old woman interrupted the silence, "The street name is Brøndby?"

"Yes." I wondered how she just knew the street name. I said, "How did you know?"

"There are only two main streets in our neighborhood."

Then, she paused a moment and said, "What is the number of your friend's house?"

I said, "Seven."

She said, "Well, then."

As we got off the bus, the old woman stretched her hand out to the distance, pointing to a group of far-flung houses at the hem of the mountains, lush and pristine, as though no human had ever set a foot on their paths. She said, "This is the Taastrup neighborhood."

The old woman walked briskly ahead of me, suddenly excited, almost running, through the damp, fine, cool grass. I followed, languid, contemplative, gloomy, perturbed, pouting that no one had come to welcome me; my eyes roved over the houses. From a distance, I read the sign nailed to the street's forehead: TAASTRUP, BRØNDBY STREET.

Following her footsteps, I stepped, suddenly excited and light-footed myself, onto Brøndby Street and felt a smile fall onto my lips, completely restoring me: body, heart, and soul. I was elated, as if some second soul had entered my body.

Then, I noticed the old woman standing at a garden

gate, fitting a key into the lock. When I caught up to her, she was opening the gate. With a shining, comforting smile, she asked, "Is your friend's name Birgitte?"

I couldn't help but wonder, "How did you know?"

With her left hand, she pushed open the gate and said, "Welcome to the Taastrup neighborhood, Brøndby Street, House No. 7. Here! Be my guest."

As if spellbound, baffled, and flustered, my eyes roved over the door. There it was: No. 7, Brøndby Street!

So, she and I—we became friends. She welcomed me through the open door.

I walked inside with my backpack, stunned.

The old woman welcomed me once more and said, "Please, sit."

On the left-hand side of the lawn, I found a chair and sat down. The old woman disappeared. I said to myself, "Well, then, her name is Birgitte." She emerged once more and handed me a glass of water. Before I took a sip, I asked, "Are you really Birgitte Poulsen?"

The old woman took out her ID and handed it to me. I looked it over: Birgitte Poulsen. Retired teacher. Born 1938—Skagen. Taastrup neighborhood, Brøndby Street, House No. 7. The same name and address I read in that corner of the personals, the same name and address that brought me here from Copenhagen. I said, "But the picture in the advertisement was of a young woman!"

"That picture, that picture was of me in my youth. I used that picture on purpose."

"Why?"

"If I hadn't done that, would you have come to meet me?"

I drank the water and handed the glass back to her.

The old woman, satisfied, picked up the tray, put the glass on it, and said, "I'll be right back."

I watched her leave, taking in her luscious curves. I had the sudden desire to chase those luscious, white-hot curves into the house and ride them.

I thought, "So, what's the problem? So many of my friends, Maghdid and Zhilwan and Abdulla and Saman . . . all live with older women in their fifties or sixties, why shouldn't I? Agh, perhaps all of us, a generation of young refugees in Europe will live in the margins, the margins of Europe."

I pitied myself, "For almost two years, in Copenhagen, in loneliness and solitude, I stewed and rotted. Birgitte is a merciful, educated woman . . . at least to learn the language . . . then, that's that . . . I'll live with her . . ."[9]

---

9. Kurdo had bought a return ticket. Deliberately, he pulled the ticket out from his pocket and tore it up.

—

When the old woman came back out to the lawn, Kurdo was still sitting on the chair, his elbows on the table in front of him, head in his hands, looking at the scraps of the ticket he had torn up.

Paris-Hawler
1993–1999

The Deserter

I SAT IN THE TEAHOUSE, settling back into a chair, to rest a while. All of a sudden, I realized: I'd left my right leg back at the base.

Nothing like this had ever happened to me; all my life, I'd never forgotten my leg anywhere. As I stood up to leave, I shocked the waiter, a dark-skinned Arab man from the south of Iraq.

"You walked!" he shouted.

"Yes, but still!" I said.

"What?"

"I left my right leg back at the base."

At that, the waiter laughed. "How many years have you been a soldier?"

"Just a couple months."

"Well, that makes sense. You'll get used to it."

So, lame and limping on my one leg, I made it back to the base. After a while waiting outside our officer's quarters, they called me in. Out of breath, I saluted our officer and said, "Sir, I'm sorry, I have forgotten my right leg in the training area."

The officer, irate, bellowed, "Don't bother me with this shit. Go see your corporal."

I went to our corporal. I said the same; he did the same: "Go see your sergeant."

Our sergeant's full name was Rob M. Blind, but everyone just called him Sergeant Blind. He was as polished a man as you can imagine. He took me to a massive armory, dark and full of human hands and legs, heads and noses and ears, thighs and backs, even fingers, and said, "Have a look."

I searched the armory high and low but couldn't find my missing leg. I felt so bereft, I thought I might split in two. "What now?" I asked.

"You must not have left it in the training area," he said.

"No. This afternoon, before we began training, I had it."

"No," he insisted sternly, "you didn't leave it on the base."

"Yes, I did."

"Don't lie. You must have lost it somewhere else."

Locking the armory, he said, "Go home for the night. Tomorrow, we'll track it down."

Tomorrow and the day after and the day after that, I searched and found no trace of it. And so, for nine days, I reported for duty, looked for my leg and refused to choose a stranger's. On the tenth day, they said, "In southern Iraq, we're fighting off our enemy's new major offensive; you deploy tomorrow."

"But I can't go. I don't have a right leg."

"Never mind. We'll get you a leg."

Sergeant Blind came with me once again to the dark armory. He pulled a leg out from among a heap of human hands and legs and chests and thighs. He handed it to me and said, "Here! Try it on."

I tried the leg on. It was so short. I said, "This leg isn't for me, sir! It's too short."

He got out another leg, dark-skinned, long, and hairy. He handed it to me, saying, "How's this one?"

I glanced at it. "Sir, this leg is entirely too long, it won't fit me."

This time he hauled out another leg—bloodied and riddled with bullet holes—that had rotted black. "Here," he said, "This one!"

Hoping to use my missing leg as an excuse to keep me from the trenches, I said, "Sir! This leg is rank and perforated with bullet holes."

At this, the sergeant finally lost his temper. He plucked his own head off his shoulders, slammed it down on the table in front of him, and said, "Look! Me, even my head is not my own. But tomorrow, like you, I must report to the trenches."

Then he grabbed his head and shoved it back in place. He elaborated, aggravated, and angered, "You're only missing your right leg, yet in war, you see only conscription, not service."

Taking in his diatribe, I felt for the sergeant. I suddenly couldn't bear to face him. I didn't know what to say. He continued, complaining as if to a friend, and I found myself listening intently, "All you Kurds are like this. Always holding yourself apart from us Arabs."

His words made me blush. In my gut, I knew: It was a shame to let him think I was using my missing leg as an excuse to avoid battle, to let him perceive Kurds as cowards, to let him believe we fear fighting. So I said, "Sir, take heart!" I forced myself to hold out my hand for a leg. "Forget it. Just give me a leg!"

"Which one?"

"Any one."

When I got home, I went to pack my clothes and gear. Tomorrow I'd be sent to the front lines. Then I noticed my missing leg had sent me a letter. Bewildered and so happy I was downright giddy, I opened the letter.

My missing right leg wrote that some days ago, in the city's bazaar, police asked him for ID; because he was unable to produce any papers, the cops thought him a deserter and decided, since he was a deserting Kurd, they would send him straight to the front lines. He seized his chance to evade custody, fled the cops, and lost them, dodging and racing through the bazaar. He didn't stop until he got to Baghdad where he obtained a fake ID, went to the Kindi Terminal and then, by bus, returned to Hawler.

My missing right leg, with his hurried letter, shocked me, body and soul. I wondered how my lone, hamstrung leg had such courage, how he had gotten himself back to Hawler. Most shocking of all: In the letter, my leg asked me to desert, as he had, and join him back in Hawler. In a cramped, unruly hand, he wrote: "I'm begging: Come back. I can't live without you. As soon as possible, desert and come back to Hawler! Together, here, we'll figure something out: We can go to Iran or Turkey, and from there we can reach Europe. From then on, together, in Europe, we'll live well, we'll finally be content . . . "

Come back . . . as soon as possible . . . I can't live without you . . .

The letter's words reverberated inside my skull.

A cold sweat gripped my entire body. I sat in my room, head as heavy as if two skulls hung in my hands, legions of weary thoughts tramping around inside my mind.

'*Come back . . . as soon as possible . . . we can reach Europe!*'

I kept thinking; I, my soul, my head, my very skull were all beyond tired, too tired to desert, to have the courage to go through Turkey and from there make it to Europe. I, with my brief twenty-nine years, I had this thought: "So, maybe I'll lose my life and future in this disastrous, absurd war, but why risk them on some other barren gambit of inevitable grief?" I sat down on a chair in my room, took out a paper and pen, and started writing a letter to my lovely right leg. My heart heavy with desire, melancholy, and nostalgia, my eyes blurred with tears, I wrote:

> O, my lovely right leg! Forgive me; my soul is spent. Perhaps you know this well: I constantly desert my own life and any sense of the future. Always, I desert myself. I have run out of courage. I can't enjoy life's delights or beauty anymore, not at home, not in Europe. My generation and I—desperate, ill-fated youth—we are the sacrifice of our time, the sacrifice that these idiots and asses we call leaders today make

to the filthy gods of war. I'm just so tired, so very, very tired. If you do take off for Europe, go, Godspeed! I wish you only the best and every happiness . . .

1989

Lamartine

IN PARIS, FOR SIX OR SEVEN MONTHS, I had been looking for a job. One day, only twenty francs in my pocket, I
went to the unemployment office, the ANPE. I thought
maybe I could get a job I could actually live on.

In the waiting room, a group of others: French and not,
girl, boy, white, black, red, we sat and waited. After waiting almost an hour, my turn came, and I went into the next
room. A woman sat behind a desk. "Welcome," she said.

I sat down. I showed her my ID. I said, "I don't have a
job. I came here hoping to find one."

She reached for my ID and perused my documents
in a file she had in front of her. "You graduated from the
Sorbonne..."

"Yes."

Her face softened. She asked, "With a specialty in which field?"

"In rhyme," I said.

The woman, bewildered, fell silent. After a moment, she said, "Rhyme?"

"Yes, in poetry."

She raised her head, studying the mass of clouds gathering in the room, and said, "What did you study?"

I said, "I have a doctorate."

"In . . ."

"The rhymes of Lamartine's poetry."

"And what job do you want?"

"Any job I can live on."

I thought I'd angered the woman because she immediately retorted, "We can't find those kinds of jobs for people like you."

I was baffled. "Why is that?"

She said, "Every unemployed person who comes to this agency seeking work must at least have some expertise in some field!"

I got impatient. "Yes, ma'am, as I told you: I have extensive expertise in rhyme. I dedicated four years of my life to the process of studying and digging into rhyme. I've even published some on the subject."

The woman once more fell silent. After another moment, she said, "Yes, but have you ever worked?"

This question worried me a little, but I didn't let it show. I said, "Yes, ma'am, and how!"

"Doing what?"

"Ma'am, all my adult life, for nearly eleven years, I have written poetry. I have extensive expertise in writing poetry. This is why I chose to pursue my doctoral degree in the rhyme schemes of Lamartine's poetry."

"So, you became a specialist in rhyme!"

"Yes, ma'am. In the rhyme schemes of Lamartine's poems."

Just then, a cat jumped onto the desk. The woman glanced at me and said, "Cats don't bother you?"

I glanced at the cat and said, "Not at all."

The woman retrieved a flower from her desk drawer, savored its smell, then steadily moved on, "Okay! A branch of our agency buys and sells poems, but . . ."

"But what, ma'am?"

"For this kind of work, we have some conditions."

"What conditions, ma'am?"

The woman stroked the cat to the end of its tail, looked at the papers before her, and said, "First of all, we must read the cats!"

"You mean the poems?"

"Yes. We must love them. The second condition is actually the most important: The day you give your poems to our agency, you must deposit thirteen thousand francs."

"And what is this deposit of thirteen thousand francs for, ma'am?"

"In the event the committee doesn't love the poems, they will return half your deposit."

"And if they do love them?"

"Then of course, they'll pay for them."

"How much per kilogram?"

"We don't buy by the kilogram. We buy one at a time. Classic poems: five hundred francs. Free verse: three hundred francs. Prose poems: a hundred fifty francs. Quatrains, quintains, and such: a hundred francs."

"Are there any other conditions?"

"We have a committee that meets once a year to select the poets' work. They always answer the poets, accepting or rejecting, within eight months. Each year, altogether too many people offer to sell their poems to our agency."

"Thank you," I said to the woman and, without another word, stood and left.

—

I stuffed my hands in my coat pockets. Wretched and wandering, I found myself on Saint-Germain-des-Prés. There, in a small square that boasts a statue of Lamartine, beside a kiosk, I stood still. At a little distance from the statue, as if it were my first time to see it, I studied each detail of the grand and glorious Lamartine: the great French poet of the nineteenth century, so well-tailored and stylish, seated, majestic; his right hand settled on his right knee, his left hand raised, his index finger pointed to the sky, as if mid-recitation. After a while, exhausted and heartsick, I went and sat at the feet of his statue.

Just as I sat down, at my back, Lamartine said, in a loud voice, as if he wanted to commiserate, "Don't bother worrying!"

Slouching, my head hung low, as if to myself, I murmured, "How can I not worry?"

Lamartine, behind me, at once weary and sorrowful said, "This is how it goes . . . !"

I raised my head to face the street, filled with runaway cars, coming and going, and said, as if I were just talking to myself, "If I had thirteen thousand francs and could wait eight more months, why would I go to them and beg for a job? Why would I even need a job?"

Lamartine snapped back, "To begin with, you shouldn't have trusted your fate to poetry, aesthetics, and writing!"

At these words from Lamartine, I turned on him, angry, and said, "And you? Why did you trust your fate to poetry, aesthetics, and writing?"

Just as angry, he spat back, "I was an ass!"

I fell silent. I had no answer to that. I suddenly understood: Lamartine, like me, was heartsick; he needed to blame himself, to break himself, until, if nothing else, he could bring a bit of peace to his heart.

I turned back to face the street. I said, "We really do live pitifully, we and all like us, artists and poets. I often imagine that at the beginning of time, a demon nursed us: misfortune our first milk."

Casting about, agonizing, my eyes staggered, left and right. I began to tremble in my heart and my soul and my knees.

After a moment, in a stricken voice, still loud enough for Lamartine to hear me, I said, "I'm sorry, Monsieur Lamartine, but can you lend me a hundred francs for a few days?"

My eyes were anywhere but on myself. I waited for an answer but heard nothing. After a while, I turned around and saw Lamartine wasn't there.

I looked to my left and saw Lamartine there, throwing his coat over his shoulder and walking away. I followed him.

I called after him, "Monsieur Lamartine!" He stopped in front of a café. He looked pressed. I asked, "You're leaving?"

"Yeah, it's late, I have to get to work."

"Where do you work?"

"In a hotel."

"The night shift?"

"Yeah. I'm a security guard, a night watchman at a hotel."

I wanted to ask him how much he gets paid per night, but I knew he was in a hurry and needed to get to the metro station to continue on his way to work, so I asked only, "Monsieur Lamartine, can't you ask around and maybe find me a job?"

He said, "You know, I'm alone here, a stranger. I know no one in Paris."

Surprised, I stuttered, "In Paris . . . you . . . know no one?"

"Yes, my friend, you and I belong to the nineteenth century; no one knows us. Still, for you, I'll do what I can. But goodbye for now. I have to get to work."

Lamartine left me, but a little ways down the road he turned back to call out, "If you want, come visit me some night. The hotel is close to the Cadet metro station, Trévise Street, No. 7, Prima Hotel. Goodbye for now."

Lamartine, harried, ran onto the metro. His steps faltered as time and again they turned him back to catch sight of his plinth, and all the while his steps wept, the tears falling thick and quick . . .

Paris

1991

A Refugee

ONE EVENING, A KURDISH REFUGEE IN Munich went to a café. The waiter came and asked him, "Welcome, what would you like to drink?"

The refugee replied, "Ten bananas, please!"

The waiter, a while later, brought him ten bananas in a basket that he put on the table.

The refugee, consumed by desire, ate the first banana and threw the peel onto the sidewalk, ate the second banana and threw the peel onto the sidewalk, ate the third banana and threw the peel onto the sidewalk, ate the fourth banana and threw the peel onto the sidewalk, ate the fifth banana and threw the peel onto the sidewalk, ate the sixth banana and threw the peel onto the sidewalk, ate the seventh banana and threw the peel onto the sidewalk, ate the eighth banana and threw the peel onto the sidewalk, ate the ninth banana and threw the peel onto the sidewalk, ate the tenth banana and threw the peel onto the sidewalk.

The waiter rushed back to the table, faced the refugee, and, livid, said, "Man! Why did you eat the first banana and throw the peel onto the sidewalk, eat the second banana and throw the peel onto the sidewalk, eat the third banana and throw the peel onto the sidewalk, eat the fourth banana and throw the peel onto the sidewalk, eat the fifth banana and throw the peel onto the sidewalk, eat the sixth banana and throw the peel onto the sidewalk, eat the seventh banana and throw the peel onto the sidewalk, eat the eighth banana and throw the peel onto the sidewalk, eat the ninth banana and throw the peel onto the sidewalk, eat the tenth banana and throw the peel onto the sidewalk?"

The refugee said, "And why don't I have the right to eat the first banana and throw the peel onto the sidewalk, to eat the second banana and throw the peel onto the sidewalk, to eat the third banana and throw the peel onto the sidewalk, to eat the fourth banana and throw the peel onto the sidewalk, to eat the fifth banana and throw the peel onto the sidewalk, to eat the sixth banana and throw the peel onto the sidewalk, to eat the seventh banana and throw the peel onto the side-walk, to eat the eighth banana and throw the peel onto the sidewalk, to eat the ninth banana and throw the peel onto the sidewalk, to eat the tenth banana and throw the peel onto the sidewalk?"

Meanwhile, the café owner, a fat red giant with a chevron mustache, came to mediate; he asked the waiter, "What's all this? What's this ruckus?" The waiter said, "He is a refugee! He has eaten one banana and thrown the peel onto the sidewalk, he has eaten a second banana and thrown the peel onto the sidewalk, he has eaten a third banana and thrown the peel onto the sidewalk, he has eaten a fourth banana and thrown the peel onto the sidewalk, he has eaten a fifth banana and thrown the peel onto the sidewalk, he has eaten a sixth banana and thrown the peel onto the sidewalk, he has eaten a seventh banana and thrown the peel onto the sidewalk, he has eaten an eighth banana and thrown the peel onto the sidewalk, he has eaten a ninth banana and thrown the peel onto the sidewalk, he has eaten a tenth banana and thrown the peel onto the sidewalk."

The café owner, livid, said to the refugee, "You never had the right to eat that first banana and throw the peel onto the sidewalk, to eat the second banana and throw the peel onto the sidewalk, to eat the third banana and throw the peel onto the sidewalk, to eat the fourth banana and throw the peel onto the sidewalk, to eat the fifth banana and throw the peel onto the sidewalk, to eat the sixth banana and throw the peel onto the sidewalk, to eat the seventh banana and throw the peel onto the sidewalk, to eat the eighth banana and throw the peel onto the sidewalk, to eat the ninth banana and throw the peel onto the sidewalk, to eat the tenth banana and throw the peel onto the sidewalk!" And with that, he went to call the police. The policemen busted in, all shoulders. Their ranking officer, blotchy-faced, baton in hand, said to the refugee, "Is this true? That you ate one banana and threw the peel onto the sidewalk, that you ate a second banana and threw the peel onto the sidewalk, that you ate a third banana and threw the peel onto the sidewalk, that you ate a fourth banana and threw the peel onto the sidewalk, that you ate a fifth banana and threw the peel onto the sidewalk, that you ate a sixth banana and threw the peel onto the sidewalk, that you ate a seventh banana and threw the peel onto the sidewalk, that you ate an eighth banana and threw the peel onto the sidewalk, that you ate a ninth banana and threw the peel onto the sidewalk, that you ate a tenth banana and threw the peel onto the sidewalk?"

And the refugee, since Germany had not yet granted him asylum or even an official ID, grew nervous. He knew they would catch him; with fear and trembling, he said, "No, I never ate one banana and threw the peel onto the sidewalk, never ate a second banana and threw the peel onto the sidewalk, never ate a third banana and threw the peel onto the sidewalk, never ate a fourth banana and threw the peel onto the sidewalk, never ate a fifth banana and threw the peel onto the sidewalk, never ate a sixth banana and threw the peel onto the sidewalk, never ate a seventh banana and threw the peel onto the sidewalk, never ate an eighth banana and threw the peel onto the sidewalk, never ate a ninth banana and threw the peel onto the sidewalk, never ate a tenth banana and threw the peel onto the sidewalk."

The policeman went to a woman who had been seated near the refugee in the café. He asked her, "Excuse me, ma'am, but did you see this refugee eat one banana and throw the peel onto the sidewalk, eat a second banana and throw the peel onto the sidewalk, eat a third banana and throw the peel onto the sidewalk, eat a fourth banana and throw the peel onto the sidewalk, eat a fifth banana and throw the peel onto the sidewalk, eat a sixth banana and throw the peel onto the sidewalk, eat a seventh banana and throw the peel onto the sidewalk, eat an eighth banana and throw the peel onto the sidewalk, eat a ninth banana and throw the peel onto the sidewalk, eat a tenth banana and throw the peel onto the sidewalk?" She said, "This man? Eat one banana and throw the peel onto the sidewalk, eat a second banana and throw the peel onto the sidewalk, eat a third banana and throw the peel onto the sidewalk, eat a fourth banana and throw the peel onto the sidewalk, eat a fifth banana and throw the peel onto the sidewalk, eat a sixth banana and throw the peel onto the sidewalk, eat a seventh banana and throw the peel onto the sidewalk, eat an eighth banana and throw the peel onto the sidewalk, eat a ninth banana and throw the peel onto the sidewalk, eat a tenth banana and throw the peel onto the sidewalk? No, I didn't see that."

Even so, the policeman handcuffed the refugee and rushed him off to the station in the back of a squad car. There, the station chief, sharp and crushing, said to the refugee, "You! Who do you think you are? That you eat one banana and throw the peel onto the sidewalk, that you eat a second banana and throw the peel onto the sidewalk, that you eat a third banana and throw the peel onto the sidewalk, that you eat a fourth banana and throw the peel onto the sidewalk, that you eat a fifth banana and throw the peel onto the sidewalk, that you eat a sixth banana and throw the peel onto the sidewalk, that you eat a seventh banana and throw the peel onto the sidewalk, that you eat an eighth banana and throw the peel onto the sidewalk, that you eat a ninth banana and throw the peel onto the sidewalk, that you eat a tenth banana and throw the peel onto the sidewalk?"

And the refugee, yelling at the top of his lungs, said: "No, no, I'm not crazy! How could I make such a mistake? To eat one banana and throw the peel onto the sidewalk, to eat a second banana and throw the peel onto the sidewalk, to eat a third banana and throw the peel onto the sidewalk, to eat a fourth banana and throw the peel onto the sidewalk, to eat a fifth banana and throw the peel onto the sidewalk, to eat a sixth banana and throw the peel onto the sidewalk, to eat a seventh banana and throw the peel onto the sidewalk, to eat an eighth banana and throw the peel onto the sidewalk, to eat a ninth banana and throw the peel onto the sidewalk, to eat a tenth banana and throw the peel onto the sidewalk!"

The next day, journalists in their newspapers published report after report, article after article on this incident, and each one, under its bold headline, detailed how a Kurdish refugee in a Munich café ordered ten bananas and then ate one banana and threw the peel onto the sidewalk, ate a second banana and threw the peel onto the sidewalk, ate a third banana and threw the peel onto the sidewalk, ate a fourth banana and threw the peel onto the sidewalk, ate a fifth banana and threw the peel onto the sidewalk, ate a sixth banana and threw the peel onto the sidewalk, ate a seventh banana and threw the peel onto the sidewalk, ate an eighth banana and threw the peel onto the sidewalk, ate a ninth banana and threw the peel onto the sidewalk, ate a tenth banana and threw the peel onto the sidewalk.

That evening, German TV and radio broadcast the same news: "A Kurdish refugee living in Germany for eleven years without asylum just lost his mind. Last night, in a Munich café, police saw him order ten bananas, then eat one banana and throw the peel onto the sidewalk, eat a second banana and throw the peel onto the sidewalk, eat a third banana and throw the peel onto the sidewalk, eat a fourth banana and throw the peel onto the sidewalk, eat a fifth banana and throw the peel onto the sidewalk, eat a sixth banana and throw the peel onto the sidewalk, eat a seventh banana and throw the peel onto the sidewalk, eat an eighth banana and throw the peel onto the sidewalk, eat a ninth banana and throw the peel onto the sidewalk, eat a tenth banana and throw the peel onto the sidewalk."

Paris
July 1992

An Epic Tragedy

a man . . .

a woman . . .

each their own loneliness . . .

The Potato Eaters

> If you leave, every return is as if
> You've left home to arrive in Jabulqa.
>
> —Haji Qadir Koye

FEREYDUN PUT HIS HEAD DOWN AND left his village. Then the rumors flew: Everyone said something different. Some people said, "He's gone to Germany," some said, "He's arrived in Sweden," some others said, "He's in Canada," and still others said he was camped out in Colombia, smuggling hashish. His close friends said, "In Denmark, he's gotten himself a wife, a Polish woman, and works in restaurants." His brothers and sisters, strangest of all, said, "We get his letters from America. He says he's there."

When Fereydun left, a severe plague spread through his village. People would begin to vomit involuntarily, then fall into bed for three or four days and die in complete agony. Fereydun had left, and stayed away, and for thirteen years the plague raged on.

Now, the plague spent, after thirteen years of absence, of carrying his home on his shoulders, he has returned to his village.

Fereydun returned home as if just coming back from the teahouse, like any other evening, except he held a bag, an immense, full bag.

Fereydun hadn't heard: The villagers, throughout thirteen years of plague, had let many customs and traditions slip through their fingers only to take hold of new standards and ethics, the strangest of which was their potato-eating habit. As hunger became famine, long after Fereydun had left, eating potatoes became a habit.

People, little by little, as the plague spread, lost their taste for anything else; year by year, more and more, any other food came to disgust them: They ate only potatoes. Every crop and harvest: only potatoes. In the plains, in kitchen gardens, beside every gate, even in teahouses and schools, they planted only potatoes. They drank potato water. The more fortunate drank potato juice. Aghas, efendis, and noblemen drank potato beer and potato wine and potato arak. The poor, they preserved potato water in winter to drink in summer. People dressed in tailored potato peels. They hung pictures of potatoes of all shapes and sizes on the walls of their homes and teahouses. And their Ramadan offerings and general tithes were potatoes. The most coveted gift for a housewarming or solstice or any given week or occasion was only the potato. When someone died, they washed the body with potato water and, in the end, laid a single potato to rest in the grave.

Fereydun's brothers and sisters, his father, and all their relatives were so happy at Fereydun's return that despite their poverty, they threw a party that very day, a party for family, old friends, and even acquaintances that lasted three nights and three days. They danced and celebrated to drums, the zurna, and various bands.

Throughout these three nights and three days, reporters from all the big-city radio and television stations, newspapers and magazines, one after the other, came to interview Fereydun. Such-and-so party radio station blared, "A titan of a poet has returned to our homeland." Such-and-so party television channel declared, "A Kurdish student graduated from a famous university in the United States and returned to his village." Newspapers and magazines splashed it across their headlines, "A talented writer returned to his birthplace to serve his own nation."

So, for three nights and three days, between all the respect and propaganda, Fereydun became "the greatest poet, the humblest master, the most famous writer" in his country.

So, for three nights and three days, Fereydun had his hands full. Fereydun's family and relatives constantly invited him to their homes. Poor households borrowed potatoes from their wealthy relatives so they could invite Fereydun over. And the village aghas, noblemen, and efendis invited him out for potato beers or other potato drinks at their private clubs. Close and distant acquaintances, when they visited him, each offered him a gift: a single painted potato in a paper sack.

Fereydun, at first himself, gradually, over the course of these three days, became somewhat accustomed to potatoes; he ate and drank only potatoes as if this were normal.

On the fourth night, at eleven thirty P.M., his father and sisters and brothers, his brothers- and sisters-in-law and all their kids, his maternal and paternal uncles and all their kids, his aunt and her kids, sat all together in Fereydun's father's living room; their potato dinner eaten, they gathered around Fereydun.

—

His father turned to Fereydun and said, "Now, then, Fereydun, my son! What have you brought for us?"

This question delighted Fereydun. So happy that he felt giddy, Fereydun thought, "This will be such a surprise!" He stood, so proud, and placed the bag with its immense fullness in the dead center of the room, before his father, and let its contents spill out.

The bag, like a sack of wheat, split open and fine gold, like bright yellow flour, sifted down, then more fell, the pieces getting bigger and bigger until they were the size of bricks. Fereydun, thrilled, proud, and happy, watched that shimmering gold fall as if it were the sweat of his soul, exhausted from the thirteen years of his exile, and said, "Here, my beloved father! I brought you gold."

His sister-in-law, breastfeeding her frail newborn, asked, "This bag, it's all just gold?"

Fereydun replied, "Yes, it's all gold."

His sister, bewildered, in a slightly raised voice, asked again, "It's all just gold?"

Fereydun said, "Yes. It's all just gold."

His maternal uncle, more confused than anyone else, asked, "It's all just gold?"

Fereydun said, "Yes, all just gold."

His father threw in, "So, you didn't bring any potatoes from abroad?"

Fereydun said, "No. I didn't bring any potatoes from abroad."

His elder brother, shocked, raised his voice, "You didn't bring any potatoes from abroad?!"

Fereydun was more surprised and bewildered than them. "No, I didn't bring any potatoes from abroad."

His brother-in-law said, "Really? You didn't bring any potatoes from abroad?"

"No," he replied, "I didn't bring any potatoes from abroad."

His maternal uncle, confused and a little angry, said, "Really? Really? You didn't bring any potatoes from abroad?"

"No, I didn't bring any potatoes from abroad."

His paternal uncle, as if he wanted to grab him by the collar and shake him, said, "You're serious? You brought not one potato from abroad?"

Fereydun, still somewhat confused, but calm, said, "Yes, I'm serious, I didn't bring any potatoes from abroad."

His cousin from his father's sister, said, "So, seriously, you didn't bring any potatoes from abroad?"

Fereydun began to hyperventilate. "Yes, seriously, I didn't bring any potatoes from abroad."

His aunt said, "I mean, how is it possible you brought not one potato from abroad?"

Fereydun was getting angry. "I didn't bring any potatoes from abroad."

His cousin from his father's brother, said, "Well, but how? Why didn't you bring any potatoes from abroad?"

Fereydun felt like he was defending a mistake he'd made or some crime he'd committed. "I don't know. I didn't bring any potatoes from abroad."

His cousin, from his mother's brother, said, "Well, that's strange! Why didn't you bring any potatoes from abroad?"

Fereydun, calmly: "Why is that strange? I didn't bring any potatoes from abroad."

Fereydun's father, at last, with sorrow and grief, took a tragic, desperate breath: "Well, but why, my son? Why didn't you bring any potatoes with you?"

Fereydun, mustering his pride at the thought of the great value of the gold, said, "I brought only gold with me."

His maternal uncle, a dark-skinned, broad-shouldered

man with a sweeping handlebar mustache, with curiosity, wondered aloud, "What is gold, my boy?"

Fereydun, given the heated back-and-forth, finally understood that no one in his family remembered what gold was. That no one else in the village now could or would understand the value of gold. Agh. Ugh. He refused to feel like a failure or an idiot, but when he considered trying to explain to them the value and worth of gold, it seemed a hardship, almost hopeless. So, with sorrow and that hopelessness, sinking into the absurdity of it all, he looked into his maternal uncle's ignorant eyes and fell silent.

His sister-in-law, her frail newborn in her embrace, got to her feet, said "Pfff!", and left. As she walked out, she threw a snarl of words. "Thirteen years he lived abroad, and what did he bring back, not one sack of potatoes!"

His aunt, the wife of his maternal uncle, tossed the cigarette from her fingers, got to her feet, said "Indeed . . . Pfff!", and walked out as well, saying, "Thirteen years we haven't seen him and he brings us not even one potato sack as a gift!"

His aunt, the wife of his paternal uncle, quietly got to her feet, took her child's hand, and also left, mumbling desperately on her way out, "Bah . . . What the hell is this? You didn't bring a single potato with you!"

His brother-in-law, sighing and complaining, left without

a glance at Fereydun, mumbling, "If nothing else, you could have brought just a few potatoes as gifts for the kids!"

His aunt, the fattest of them all, arriving late, stood at the threshold only to mumble and grumble in the court-yard, "People coming back from abroad always bring sacks of potatoes with them, but he brings this useless shit . . . no one but him even knows what it is!"

All his cousins—mother's brother's kids, father's broth-er's kids, father's sister's kids—all his nieces and nephews, his uncles, paternal and maternal, continuously, one after the other, stood and left the room desperately; quietly, as they turned their backs on him, they'd say, "Thirteen years you lived abroad, and you didn't even bring a few potatoes with you!"

"Thirteen years you lived abroad, and you didn't even bring a few potatoes with you!"

"Thirteen years you lived abroad, and you didn't even bring a few potatoes . . . "

"Thirteen years you lived abroad, and you didn't even bring . . . "

"Thirteen years you lived abroad, and you didn't . . . "

"Thirteen years you lived abroad . . . "

His elder sister, with an old scar on her temple, which people whispered came from the claw of the village's mythical eagle, felt a lump in her throat, then fell to weeping, as if something inside her were breaking, and said, "Dear Fereydun! I wish you hadn't disgraced and humiliated us so." And she took her child's hand and left.

His younger brother, with fury and a stare like a rock loosed from a slingshot, mocked him. "What is 'gold'?" Then, with unleashed fury, and no little disquiet, he stormed out.

His elder brother, a gentler, more intellectual man, stood and went to Fereydun. He leaned down to his brother, eyes brimming with tears, a tangle of sorrowful words falling out of his mouth. "Dear Fereydun! If nothing else, you could have brought just a few potatoes for us. Didn't you know how bad we have it? Didn't you know? Didn't you know we're barely getting by?"

Fereydun crumpled like a corpse. His head hung between his knees. Silent, in shock, he tried to think. He looked as if he'd been abandoned in a desert and fallen into a fever dream, he was so unaware of his surroundings.

Still, after all, there was their father, downcast, defeated, stunned. He looked toward the collapsed sack of gold in the middle of the room as if it were the remains of a loved one; as a reproach, he asked, "Well, son, but what is gold? What's it good for?"

—

Fereydun, raising his head, abruptly discovered himself in a desolate, deserted room. His head throbbed, the way a long party makes one go deaf. But he was happy that all of them had left, left him alone, the room finally empty. He got to his feet and took tearful steps toward the photograph of his late mother centered on the far wall: his mother, who, during the plague, the period of Fereydun's absence, had passed away; his mother, whom he'd never see again; his mother, who hadn't been here today, this evening; who wasn't here, sadly, to pull Fereydun into her arms, to rest his deaf head on her tender chest and comfort him. His mother: the only person left in their country, in their village, who still understood the value of gold, who still remembered its worth, the only person who knew what gold was, resting now in a freezing grave.

Hawler

1995–9

Schizophrenia

[1]

Bakhtiyar stood, captive, hapless, in front of the officer handling his case.

The officer turned to Bakhtiyar's interpreter and said, "Il faudrais qu'il aille à l'hôpital psychiatrique."

The interpreter, a young Lebanese Kurd, dejected, relayed the words: "Man, I think they are going to send you to the loony bin for a while."

---

1. If you want to know who Bakhtiyar is, see box No. 11.

2. Would you like to know what happened to Bakhtiyar? See box No. 5.

[2]

Each morning, Bakhtiyar's mother took the bus from their village to the city center, where she served wealthy families: washing their clothes, sweeping their courtyards, cleaning their rooms. Three days a week (Tuesdays, Wednesdays, and Thursdays), she also went to Hawler's sanitorium, where she worked a second job also as a cleaner.

Bakhtiyar's father had been captured when the civil war first broke out, but Bakhtiyar had known nothing of it until the day a letter arrived and he read the news.

---

1. Would you like to know what Bakhtiyar's reaction was on hearing this news? See box No. 7.
2. If you would like to know what Bakhtiyar's household was saying about him, see box No. 8.

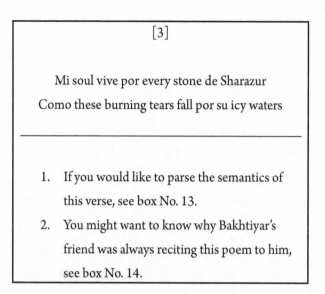

[3]

Mi soul vive por every stone de Sharazur
Como these burning tears fall por su icy waters

---

1. If you would like to parse the semantics of this verse, see box No. 13.
2. You might want to know why Bakhtiyar's friend was always reciting this poem to him, see box No. 14.

[4]

For two years, three months, and fourteen days, Bakhtiyar had been waiting in the refugee camp.

One night—after the second time the asylum office ignored his petition—at three A.M., he rose, sleepwalking, and went outside: On the street, he shattered every shop window first with stones, then, to be thorough, with a long metal pipe, too.

In the morning, Bakhtiyar, came to in the police station. He said, "I would never do anything like that. I have no idea how that happened."

---

1. If you want to know what the police did, see box No. 1.
2. If you would like to acquaint yourself with the view from Bakhtiyar's hospital room, see box No. 9.

[5]

Hearing this, Bakhtiyar instantly froze, though desperate to run.

---

1. If you would like to know why they called Bakhtiyar to the station, see box No. 14.
2. If you would like to know whether Bakhtiyar ended up in the loony bin or not, see box No. 7.

[6]

"If you recover, would you want to go home?"

"With all my heart. I long to get back to my mother's arms."

---

1. If you want to become more familiar with Bakhtiyar's mother's life, see box No. 2.
2. If you want to read a beautiful verse of poetry about this, see box No. 3.

[7]

Bakhtiyar, his heart heavy, so anxious he hadn't tended to his hair or beard in five days, found his way back to the camp, to his doorstep, and came face-to-face with a friend of his, a fellow Kurd and refugee. His friend said, "Ah . . . Bakhtiyar?"

Bakhtiyar, resentful, muttered, "My heart is almost broken. I must get back."

"Where?"

"Kurdistan."

"Why?"

"It's either that or the loony bin for me."

---

1. If you want to know something about Bakhtiyar's past, see box No. 12.

2. Do you want to know who Bakhtiyar was? See box No. 11.

[8]

Bakhtiyar's mother, his sisters, his two brothers, his aunts, his maternal uncles, his whole family . . . all of them envied Bakhtiyar. "I wish I were Bakhtiyar," they said. "He made it to Europe!"

One day, Bakhtiyar's mother, in the sanitorium, put her arm around a patient, offering him some water. The patient was a young Arab man from Al-Diwaniyah who ran to Kurdistan to escape Baghdad's Ba'athist regime. He couldn't go home. Bakhtiyar's mother pitied that young man, even though she knew that now, little by little, he was improving. She asked him:

---

1. If you want to know what Bakhtiyar's mother asked that Arab man, see box No. 6.
2. If you want to know a dream Bakhtiyar's mother had about Bakhtiyar, see box No. 4.

[9]

"This is no loony bin. Just a sanatorium to tend to mental patients. The Lebanese interpreter got it wrong," Bakhtiyar mused happily, stretched out on the cot in a striped dishdasha.

An old French woman, a nurse in the sanatorium, pitied Bakhtiyar. One evening, during dinner, she set an orange and an apple in front of Bakhtiyar and put her arm around his shoulders. With a mother's tenderness, she asked:

---

1. If you want to know what this old woman asked Bakhtiyar, see box No. 6.
2. If you want to know why this old woman would ask Bakhtiyar this question, see box No. 14.

[10]

For a while, Bakhtiyar worked in the cemetery, as part of a crew, cleaning filth and fallen leaves off the headstones and the paths between them. He thought, "I've become a garbageman."

And then for a while, they took the crew to sweep up metro stations. Bakhtiyar, because he was penniless, couldn't get any farther away from the one thousand square meters of their camp.

His Palestinian, Sri Lankan, and Lebanese friends got by stealing coats and clothes from shops then unloading them at cut-rate prices. This is how they survived. But he found that work distasteful.

---

1. If you would like to know how and when the asylum office knew Bakhtiyar had fallen ill, see box No. 4.

2. If you would like to know more about Bakhtiyar's life today, see box No. 15.

[11]

Bakhtiyar was a refugee, from Iraq, a Kurd from the village of Gomaspan who completed his coursework at Hawler's Agricultural Institute when he was twenty-one years old.

---

1. Do you want to know which country and city Bakhtiyar lived in and how? See box No. 15.
2. Would you like to know who was in Bakhtiyar's family and how they lived? See box No. 2.

[12]

When Bakhtiyar made it to France, he was well heeled and healthy, with not even a hint of illness. Now, his friends, fellow refugees in the camp, say, "Ah, Bakhtiyar. So, this is what three years of waiting does to a man."

Bakhtiyar, when he made it to France, had it in mind to study at the College of Engineering so that from time to time he could send a few dollars home to his mother.

1. Would you like to know how Bakhtiyar's destiny played out? See box No. 7.
2. Do you want to know how Bakhtiyar's family made their living? See box No. 2.

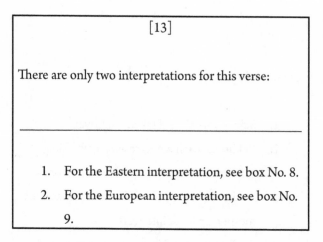

[13]

There are only two interpretations for this verse:

1. For the Eastern interpretation, see box No. 8.
2. For the European interpretation, see box No. 9.

[14]

For the below reasons:

1. Schizophrenia had taken Bakhtiyar.
2. Bakhtiyar, each night, rose, sleepwalking, shattering every shop window with stones.
3. Bakhtiyar so severely and ardently missed his mother, he burst into tears.
4. Bakhtiyar, when taken, would always insult the Kurdish political parties, saying: "They dictated my fate to be here." Even worse, he insulted, as rudely as possible, the French people and their government.

---

1. If you would like to learn more on Bakhtiyar's life in exile, see box No. 10.
2. If you want to know something about Bakhtiyar's past, see box No. 12.

[15]

Bakhtiyar lived in a village south of Paris, in an eleven-story refugee camp. He had been waiting for three years to get residency.

Sure, they gave him breakfast, lunch, and dinner, but just that. No money for cigarettes, no money for commuters' tickets.

His whole life in one square kilometer, his whole life just waiting . . . When will they grant his residency?

In the same camp, Bakhtiyar had a Kurdish friend, who claimed he was a poet.

At nightfall, he would always recite a poem of Nali's for Bakhtiyar, which begins:

---

1. If you would like to read the verse, see box No. 3.
2. If you want to become more familiar with Bakhtiyar's life in exile, see box No. 10.

Paris-Hawler

The Lion

STANDING AT THE WINDOW OF HIS ROOM, a chill breeze tousling his hair, he spared a glance for the snow piling up on the sill and sighed, "That's it then. This is my life now: always this cold and wretched wandering from this little room to the rooftop and from the rooftop back inside, like a prisoner." His fellow refugees, people he considered friends, from Sri Lanka, Chile, Iran, and Lebanon, who had lived isolated out here for months before he even arrived, told him it could be nearly a year living like this on the island; after that, God only knows which far-flung city of this Arctic country they might dispatch him to.

Just then, he heard a ship's whistle: Little by little, until it came into view from his window, the ship edged away from the island's shore. It was their island's ferry, leaving, like every other evening, loaded with refugees headed to Copenhagen

(Copenhagen!), another cold and empty island like this one. And just what would he do if he went to Copenhagen? Who would he see?

Standing at his room's window, he watched the ship splashing and spuming away, little by little drawing away from their shore. Irritable, currycombing his own heart, he muttered, "Really. So what if I go to Copenhagen? What can I do there? Who do I know? Who knows me?"

Just a few days ago, he'd had this gut feeling: "You shouldn't just sit in this room. Come on. You should get away from this island for a little while, like everyone else. If nothing else, go get some fresh air." So, with other refugees, from Lebanon, Sri Lanka, and Poland, he got on the ferry and went to Copenhagen.

The ship docked at Copenhagen's Vesterport at three thirty in the afternoon. As he disembarked, he calculated that he had, like every other refugee, until six thirty in the evening (so three hours) until he must be waiting again at the port to catch the boat and return to his island to eat dinner and sleep.

When he reached Copenhagen's bazaar, at four o'clock in the afternoon, he had no idea where to go or what to do. He searched and sauntered down the city center's streets, same as during his first visit to Copenhagen's bazaar, same as his second visit, same as his third, same as every time he'd come: lonely, no cash, no currency, a stranger, a wandering child, his eyes searching the stores and their colorful displays, his glance lingering on the golden six- and eleven-story apartment buildings. Eager, thirsty, he loosed the sling of his glance at the strawberry-blond, silken-haired girls when he could. And when he tired, he sat down on a cold garden bench. Rested, he stood to walk once more, eyes roving, exploring until he exhausted himself again. And in the end, when he made it back to the walking district along the shore, to Vesterport, he felt a fatal strangeness and solitude. A strangeness and solitude that gnawed noisily on his innermost soul. And back on the ship, on the way back to the island, he heard the refugees, some in broken English, others in Farsi and Arabic, insulting the Danish people, spitting on Denmark's weather. One of the Iranian refugees, who seemed more educated than all of them, turned to a Lebanese refugee and said in English, "Ibn Battuta, on page 285 of his travel journal, wrote, 'Denmark has foul language, foul weather, and foul manners.'"

The raucous, foul-mouthed refugees filled him with disgust; not even back in the island's cramped dining hall, not even mid-bite did they leave off from their fighting, rioting, and insulting. So strange. So, really, why had Miss Anneli, the supervisor of the island's refugees, commented the other night, "You have a lovely name"? So strange. Miss Anneli, as soon as they met, with her lovely smile, approached him to ask, "What's your name?"

He had said, "Sherzad."

Miss Anneli, always curious, then asked, "'Sherzad' and does that mean anything in Kurdish?"

"Yes."

"And what does it mean?"

"A lionhearted man."

I still don't get it. That woman, why did she say, "You have a lovely name"? Was she just trying to show a refugee kindness? Yes, perhaps, so that at least, for a moment or two, the clouds of the disquiet and foreignness he felt would clear.

Miss Anneli, before the evening she commented on his name, had glanced at him a few times with growing curiosity. The first time, he had stood alone on the beach, leaning against an old shipwreck, dispirited, despondent, gazing at the far-flung horizon of the Baltic sea, his eyes brimming with foreignness. Suddenly, Miss Anneli brushed past him, taking in his sorrow-racked posture with eyes that held questions, compassion, and mercy. The second time, he was on the building's rooftop, once again on his own, a thick, black coat draped over his shoulders. He sat on some piled gravel, huddled against the cold, head bowed as he contemplated a feeble, bony chicken pecking the ground beside the gravel, searching for worms or grain. Just then, Miss Anneli passed by with a sisterly glance, full of compassion, and the loveliest smile. Yes, it all comes down to this: people in various states of loneliness and brokenness and misery getting pitied by others.

Agh! Poor Sherzad! Twenty-nine years! Twenty-nine years full of comfort, courage, and love, twenty-nine years he had lived, full of delight and pride . . . and so, that's, well, that's that . . . today, on this far-flung island, far from his country, far from his childhood, far from the paradise of his youth, miserable, he weeps over his solitude and brokenness! Agh! A sigh of remorse escaped him as he hung his head and left the window to sit at the table in the middle of the room.

There was a small mirror on the table propped up next to an apple and a slice of grilled chicken. Today, in the dining hall at lunch, as at every other meal, he couldn't help but be disgusted by the refugees' constant riot. A Lebanese refugee, at the table, picked a fight with a Sri Lankan refugee. They fell on each other, a fight broke out, and though he knew he couldn't finish his salad, he packed his slice of grilled chicken and his apple in Saran wrap, put them in a bag, and got up. He took them back to his room and put them on the table.

Sitting, silent, he stared at the slice of chicken and the apple in front of him. Suddenly, he grinned.

Suddenly, he was a kid again! He saw himself clearly walking through their orchard with his mother. A naughty boy, as he walked, he kicked the apples that had fallen, whatever his feet could reach. His mother scolded him tenderly, "Sherzad, my boy, this is a sin! Stop kicking the apples!"

And here, now, today, after all those many years, on this Arctic island in the middle of nowhere, his daily lunch is always a slice of chicken and just one single apple! Just a single apple!

He planted his elbows on the table. His claws, this side and that, clutched at his skull. As he looked back, a sob caught in his throat. He raised his head and looked at himself in the small mirror on the table: a tangle of hair, a fistful of beard, two thick, drooping eyebrows slowly growing together... and his eyes, so strange! Each day more sunken.

So strange! This evening, in front of the mirror, with his disheveled appearance and his withered soul, he looked exactly like the mournful, broken lion he had seen in his village nineteen years earlier! Now he remembers it as if it were a dream. One evening, he was at home with his mother, aunt, sisters, and brothers, eating near the hearth, when a lion, a long rope trailing after him, crept into their courtyard to collapse on the porch.

His little sister's eyes, when they lit on the lion, flew open wide. She leveled a finger, pointing outside, and screamed, "Lion!"

It was the first time in their lives they'd seen such a wonder: Late one evening, a lion creeps into their courtyard to collapse on their porch! And with their father, for years gone on a journey he'd yet to return from.

His mother, when her eyes lit on the lion, sprang to her feet; she attacked the door handle, slammed the door shut, and threw the deadbolt. Then, together, they all rushed to the window. He, his mother, his aunt, and his younger siblings piled on top of each other in a tangle of questions, fears, and exclamations, each trying to get a glimpse of the lion. And the lion, exhausted, spent, and whimpering, just lay against the porch walls. In the moonlight, his muddled, dirty mane managed to shine. Blood leaked from his forehead and both temples and from his skull, down around his ears, viscous anguish drip, drip, dripped.

How strange! It seemed the lion had come from a long way off and saw their porch as a peaceful shelter where he could rest a while. Perhaps he had been driven away by others. From time to time, with his bloody mane, he shook himself. He chafed feebly against his rope, his limbs shaking, but couldn't rid himself of it.

Agh! Now, here, on this island, Sherzad imagines himself as the lion of his childhood. Agh! In his entire life, he had never seen himself so miserable, alone, and broken. His aunt, he remembers, had pressed herself up against the glass, almost putting herself through it, to see the lion. She said, "This lion . . . must be, war broke him."

His mother, as if begging for mercy, said, "A lion so dispirited and powerless? So faint? So miserable? Let me see no more."

His little brother, all in a rush, asked his mother, "What is that long rope wrapped around his neck?"

And his little sister, whose fear hadn't yet faded, said, "Mother . . . he must have escaped some prison."

For almost half an hour, they stood beside the window and contemplated the lion. And the lion on the porch stayed sprawled in the same spot; he didn't dare—he couldn't even—lift his head to look around. From time to time, he waved his front paws weakly around his head, trying to shoo away the flies that had settled on the bloody wounds at his temples—and even at that, he sometimes failed, flies still buzzing around his head and swarming his wounds. From time to time, he changed flanks, settling down once more with a wounded sigh.

In the end, his mother could no longer bear the sight; she stood with sudden resolve and said, "I am going to give him meat."

His aunt protested; she did not approve. His younger siblings, feeling the same, gathered around their mother, climbed into her lap, and shouted, "No, for God's sake, don't go!"

His mother said, "Enough." She bundled up a slice of grilled chicken from last night's leftovers and an apple in some Saran wrap and opened the door. "I'll just go put it in front of him," she said.

His younger siblings and aunt, all together, silent and wide-eyed, watched their mother from the window as slowly, so slowly, with hesitant steps, she approached the lion. And the lion lay still against the porch wall.

A terrible silence, springing from fear, disquiet, and shock, took hold of them all. Through the window, they saw: Their mother stood before the lion, holding out the Saran-wrapped apple and slice of chicken. Then, steadily, she bowed and placed the apple and slice of chicken on the ground.

They couldn't believe their own eyes. Open-mouthed,

agitated, in shock, they waited impatiently for their mother to come back to safety, when they could let loose their happiness and riot and laugh.

Suddenly, a strange laugh, almost a roar, rose from the window. He started, as if returning to consciousness from an otherworldly dream; exhausted and weak, he raised his head to look at the apple and slice of chicken before him, feeling fatal misgivings and misery, sorrow about to shatter him.

Mitte Grand Island

1985

The Killing of a Turkish Soldier in Zakho

The incident, as related by the efendi:

"My wife and I, with our two children, were walking across the bridge. Three Turkish soldiers were walking toward us. I took my daughter's hand. We just wanted to cross the bridge so we could see the statue of Ahmad Khani. My wife, our son in her arms, walked a few meters ahead of me. Suddenly, one of the Turkish soldiers reached out and—all I could do was watch—grabbed my wife's ass."

The incident, as related by a witness:

"Your honor, I became aware of the incident only

after suddenly, behind me, the volley of a Kalashnikov cracked and echoed. Perhaps a whole magazine. I really have no idea who shot whom! But I did see with my own eyes one soldier writhing in blood and the other two drunk; they really seemed not just drunk but wasted."

The incident, as related by the accused:

"I was aware of the whole incident, start to finish. I saw all of them from the sidewalk on the far side of the bridge. There was the efendi, his wife, and their two children. They looked like tourists, just visiting Zakho. The efendi had taken his daughter's hand, and the woman held her little boy in her arms, walking a few meters ahead of her husband. Suddenly, the Turkish soldier reached out and grabbed the woman's ass."

The incident, as related by one of the Turkish soldiers:

"The deceased, no, he made not one misstep against anyone but, on the contrary, walked across the bridge politely and, with human kindness and courtesy, gave a can of Pepsi to the efendi, the woman's husband. The catastrophe, the crime unfolded from there."

The incident, as related by the efendi:

"Yes, that's right, Your Honor, after that, I spat on the soldier. When I spat on him, he yanked the Kalashnikov off his shoulder, moving to kill me. As he pulled the Kalashnikov from his shoulder and steadied himself, he stepped a few meters back from me, my child in hand. Then, just before he fired, his soldier friend, beside him, emptied the magazine of his Kalashnikov and . . . ran off."

The incident, as related by a witness:

"Sir, as I told you: I cannot say, 'That man on the sidewalk emptied the magazine of his Kalashnikov at the soldier.' I did not see that. But when I arrived at the scene, the Kalashnikov was in the hands of the soldier who ran off and is not present here."

The incident, as related by the accused:

"I was on the sidewalk on the other side of the bridge when I saw the soldier level his Kalashnikov at the efendi. I ran to throw myself between them, so the efendi and his child would not be killed, but before I could reach the soldier, another beside him had emptied the magazine of his Kalashnikov and he was drowning in blood. It was his soldier friend who killed him. Killed him and ran off."

The incident, as related by one of the Turkish soldiers:

"When the deceased gave the can of Pepsi to the efendi, I heard the efendi, irate, say in Turkish, 'I will not drink this.' My friend said, 'Go on and drink.' The efendi, again, angrily in Turkish, said, 'I detest Turkish Pepsi. I boycott all Turkish goods, food, and drink. I never buy, eat, or drink Turkish products.' My friend asked, 'Why?' The efendi answered, 'Because you are all filthy imperialists.' My friend said, 'I apologize.' So, when we had parted ways a little, the efendi—just to anger us—shouted, in Kurdish, 'Long live Kurdistan!'"

The incident, as related by the efendi:

"How?! Yes, Your Honor, after that I spat on the soldier. Yes, my hands were full: I had my daughter."

The incident, as related by a witness:

"Yes? No, Your Honor, I am not aware whether the fallen soldier grabbed that woman's ass. Pardon me, what did you say? The soldier that ran away? I don't know. I don't know why he ran off, but he was drunk. Maybe drunken panic made him run."

The incident, as related by the accused:

"Say again, Your Honor? Yes, I saw it with my own eyes: The soldier grabbed the woman's ass. And the other soldier, unlike him, was such a man, such an honorable man, his sense of valor wouldn't allow him to stand by and just watch as someone grabbed a woman's ass and then shot her husband dead. I mean, also, he was drunk. So, Your Honor, it might not be far off to imagine he aimed his Kalashnikov at the efendi but hit his own friend! I have no idea. They were definitely drunk, though."

The incident, as related by one of the Turkish soldiers:

"The deceased did not die by his friend's hand. These two criminals are lying. They colluded to fabricate this story and claim it as the truth. Yes, that's right, the deceased was enraged when the efendi insulted the Turks and then screamed, in Kurdish, 'Long live Kurdistan,' but he didn't respond. The criminal, the man who rushed at us from the far sidewalk, insulting us, only poured fuel on the fire; he acted as if we had violated the man and woman, and he was only defending them. Even as he himself, then, lunged to grab the Kalashnikov from my friend's shoulder and kill him."

The incident, as related by the efendi:

"I swear to God: He was selfless, the man who rushed to our aid from the far sidewalk. May God hold him close. Yes, that's right: He answered for us, he wouldn't stand for Turkish soldiers assaulting us in broad daylight. But he, like me, flinched at the sudden crack of a Kalashnikov emptying its magazine. Weaponless and wronged, we never would have looked for our defense to come from his soldier friend!"

The incident, as related by a witness:

"Sir, about 'the man who rushed to their aid from the bridge's far sidewalk,' I remember only so much: After the volley, after the soldier was killed, he stood over the corpse and told the efendi, 'It was good that he was killed by one of his own.' At the same time, I saw from far off, his back to us, the runaway soldier, racing off, stumbling drunkenly."

The incident, as related by the accused:

"Your Honor, I confess: My conscience and dignity wouldn't allow me to stand by, watching helplessly, as Turkish soldiers violated a Kurdish woman and then turned to kill her husband. I ran to them, but my only intention was to come between them and the soldiers and to keep the efendi from getting killed. I've never carried a weapon."

The incident, as related by one of the Turkish soldiers:

"Your Honor, first of all, I would like to inform you that not a single one of us was drunk. And we Turks, even if we were drunk, we would not debase ourselves so much as to grab a woman's ass. Your Honor, let's say this wasn't coming from political grudge and hatred, how could one man 'grab a woman's ass,' grab a Kalashnikov, and kill a state soldier? These two men, both of them, clearly hate Turks and Turkish soldiers, and their story is obviously built of lies. They only want to protect and obscure each other's guilt."

The incident, as related by the efendi:

"Your Honor, you accuse me of starting the commotion by spitting on the Turkish soldier. I ask you only one question, Your Honor: You, if you and your wife and your two children were visiting Zakho from Hawler, on vacation, just walking across a bridge, and suddenly a Turkish soldier, as you could only watch, grabbed your wife's ass, what would you do?"

The incident, as related by a witness:

"Sir, I cannot answer this question of yours because I'm not aware of more than what I have already relayed. No, I am not aware of this issue of the can of Pepsi, nor did I see any Pepsi can at the crime scene. And also, Your Honor, I thought you took the woman's statement."

The incident, as related by the accused:

"Good God, they violate us in our own country and then accuse us and frame us as murderers! Your Honor, pardon me, but allow me to ask some questions of you: If the killer is not his soldier friend, then why did he run off? Why is he still hiding? How could you judge us, the efendi and me, under these conditions? When a critical party to the crime, the criminal, isn't here?"

The incident, as related by one of the Turkish soldiers:

"Our friend, the one who ran off, had every right to run: Before his very eyes, they emptied a Kalashnikov's entire magazine into his poor brother-in-arms. So he, maybe scared, ran. He doesn't even need to come to court, unless as a witness, because he bears no relation to this story, all lies, that these men colluded to fabricate."

The incident, as related by the efendi:

"Your Honor, my guilt and your only accusation is that I spat on the soldier. Again, please allow me a question: Your Honor, if you and your wife and your two children were visiting Zakho from Hawler, on vacation, just walking across a bridge, and suddenly a Turkish soldier, as you could only watch, grabbed your wife's ass, what would you do? What?"

The Desert

HASHUSH'S LITTLE SISTER SLAMMED THE FRONT door open, threw herself inside, and gasped, "Mama, Mama . . . tomorrow all the Kurdish families will be displaced again."

Just then, Hashush and I had sat down, facing each other, to play checkers. As Hashush heard the news, his hands fell instantly cold on the checkerboard, and the fog of sudden sorrow spread across his face. His mother quietly considered their samovar, then glanced toward me, eyes full of pity. Back then, I was just a kid and didn't speak Arabic well. I couldn't understand the slang Arabic Hashush's sister had spoken moments ago, especially because she delivered her news so rapidly.

Her news seemed to weigh heavily on Hashush's father's heart. He turned to his daughter. "Who told you this?"

The little girl, confused, glanced at me, then turned to her father, "Sa'ddiya's family, our neighbors."

"What did they say?"

"Sa'ddiya's father said it."

"What did he say exactly?"

"That tomorrow all the Kurdish families will be displaced again."

Hashush's mother turned to Hashush's father with grievous sorrow and whispered, as if speaking in secret, "She must be right. Sa'ddiya's father is a policeman; he knows."

Hashush's father muttered, "From north to south, from south now to where? What next?!"

All of a sudden, I understood, and I knew this time we would be displaced once and for all, dumped in Iran, or maybe in the deserts on Jordan's border. I almost burst into tears. How long now had my father prepared us for this? I couldn't hold the tears in any longer; beside the checkers we'd been about to play, my chin sank to my chest, and, swamped by my panic and self-pity, like a child much younger than I was at the time, I burst into tears: I had no idea why we'd been exiled to this stifling desert in the south of Iraq, or when that exile would end.

—

Next morning, confined to a room similar to a dark prison cell, as I remembered the scene from last night—how the news arrived and the confusion of Hashush's family—my heart constricted. I sat on a rusty, dented cook pot, sighing and sobbing silently. I spoke to my heart. "This is my fault. Why did I sleep over at Hashush's home?"

For exactly eleven months, my mother, father, little sister, and I had been living in this desert of southern Iraq. All told, our settlement numbered about forty or fifty Kurdish families. The Ramadi desert: devoid and bone dry, as far as the eye can see.

For the past nine years of my childhood, I had always lived at elevation, among mountains and bright gardens: The desert life of subsistence weighed heavily on me. Every dawn, I woke not to fresh breezes over our dew-covered gardens, but to dust and burning heat; I saw not my squirrel and goose and new-born kid in the lush green clearing around our house, but a yellow haze, a layer of burnt dust sprinkled on me. My mother and father and sister, they, too, felt the same longing and loss. Throughout the long eleven months we had been in the desert, only Hashush's family and some other Arab family had befriended us, only sporadically offering us help.

Every three or four days, so he could support us, my

father went with Hashush's, to I don't know which village, close to some other village, to buy radishes and return to our village to sell them.

And each morning, I went with Hashush to a dirty, remote swamp, teeming with flies and mosquitoes, to catch carp, return to the village, and sell them. And in the evenings, with Hashush and other Arab kids from the village, we met near Hashush's house, in a dry, barren sand patch where only a few scrub dates grew, giving meager shelter to a few camels hobbled beneath them each night. There, we played soccer.

I adored playing soccer. I always had plays sketched out and stuffed in my pocket. I wrote all the names of the kid players in Arabic, detailing each of their positions and roles with various symbols and lines on a piece of paper: Attacker, Defender, Goal. Many evenings, when we had exhausted ourselves playing, and night's dark wings covered the desert, Hashush and I would go to his house. Many nights I ate with them and slept over.

My mother was happy that I was playing soccer with the Arab kids. She said, "Maybe with those Arab kids, he'll pick up Arabic."

But my father, just that once, and just then, turned to me, furious, and said, "Damn you, when you're done playing, get yourself home to your own hovel and not some Arab house."

"But, Daddy, when the desert gets dark, I am afraid to cross it to get home."

"Then, damn your eyes and stop playing soccer."

'My father was right!' I thought. 'If that evening after soccer I had come back to our home and not slept over at Hashush's house, I wouldn't be separated from Mom and Dad now; and I wouldn't have stumbled into all this. Yes, it's my own fault.' In the dark, humid room, my heart was close to breaking. Through a crack in the closed door, I could see outside. I thought of my mother and my lovely little sister. I was struck by the fear that right then, with me detained in this prison cell of a room, soldiers were loading my family onto military transport trucks and dragging them to the Iranian or Jordanian borders. I would never, ever see them again!

The room they held me in, so much like a prison, was a police checkpoint, only half an hour from our house, that stood guard over that area of the desert. It was a squat cube: dark, humid, hot, smelling of piss and eggplant, the walls of cinder block and stone, patched with tin and scrap wood.

That morning, I set out from Hashush's house so early, the day's new sun had just begun to dawn, but not early enough. 'I'll be damned,' I thought, 'I'll have to take the short-cut past the checkpoint.' But when I got to the checkpoint and the Arab policeman standing guard caught sight of me, he stared as if in all his long life he'd never laid eyes on a human being moving through the desert dawn, shoul-dered his rifle, pointed the barrel right at me, and shouted in Arabic, "Don't move!"

'What have I done?' ('This is weird! It's been more than two hours. Why have they detained me in this room? What is my crime?')

When I couldn't bear one more minute, I shoved the door open and stepped outside; as I stood just by the door, the policeman quickly cocked his rifle and, carefully facing me, advanced. He puffed himself up, bellowing in Arabic slang, "Hey, orphan boy, get back in that room!"

His bellowing didn't scare me. Dread for my family sent stark pains shivering through my soul. My tongue split open. "My parents. My family!"

"So, what about your family?"

"They're leaving. They'll leave me."

He taunted me, mocking my tone, "And where would they go?"

"Won't they displace us again?"

Again, that tone, "Won't who displace you?"

I burst into tears. "The government. The government will displace us."

"And put you where?"

"Iran."

"You're lying, like I said."

"I'm not! I swear, they will displace us. I don't know where they'll put us next!"

Dismissively, he said, "Get back in that room and wait."

I knew he meant for me to wait for the commander, the commander who I knew was still asleep. Once he woke up, the policeman said, he would investigate me. At the threshold, once more I turned to the policeman, my eyes begging him to take pity. I pointed inside and said, "He's asleep."

He said, "Who is asleep?"

I said, "The commander."

He said, "Yeah, well, wait until he wakes up."

I said, "You mean I should wake him?"

His voice went taut, "No. Don't you dare! He will wake when he's ready."

I pleaded, "But he's not waking up."

He lost whatever control he had of his temper and yelled, "I said get back in that room, you little son of a bitch!"

At just that moment, I noticed another policeman I hadn't yet seen—maybe he'd just returned from visiting one of his fellow policemen. He sat in a squat, holding his rifle upright between his legs, and leaned against the wall; seeing me, he stood and came over to us. "Well, but haven't you already been displaced?"

His words gave me momentary hope. "Yes."

He said, "So, what do you mean, 'They will displace us again'?"

"They will displace us again."

"And where are you from originally?"

"Mergasur."

"And where will they displace you now?"

I cried. "I don't know . . . !"

Abruptly, he laid into me. "And where have you been at this early morning? What would someone be doing out in the desert at such an early hour?" He didn't let me respond but whipped out an ashen, wrinkled paper. I realized it was the paper I had drawn plays on, for our soccer game, and that the previous policeman had taken it from me and given it to him. He shoved the paper in my face and said in a voice ugly with anger, "So, what's this paper you have then? Huh?" His rifle strap slithered over his shoulder and he grabbed me by my elbow. "You're a spy." He tugged me closer and loomed over me, waving the paper in my face. He pointed long, cracking fingers at various points on the sketch and said, all hopped up, "Look at your own writing! Attacker, Defender, Goal . . . what is it you have written here, huh?"

This is so weird, I was thinking, *These two Arab policemen, how could they not know the basic vocabulary of a soccer game?*

He took a big pinch of my ear and twisted it. His bloated mustache brushed against me and his eyes bulged out. "What is this map you have? Talk!"

I cried.

He said, "Is it subversive?"

The sharp pain in my ear helped me answer clearly. "It is a page from a soccer play book with the names of my friends, the players, written on it."

He twisted my ear even tighter and shook my head twice, "You keep saying the same damn thing. Attacker, Defender, Goal . . . What does it mean? Attack where? What goal? What are all these strange symbols? Talk, you mole! Whose names have you written down here?"

And I had no idea what to say. I was stunned. In my misery and pain, all I could do was sob and beg. Finally, he let go of my ear, turned me by the shoulder, and shoved me inside, saying, "Go on, get in that room, sit still until the commander wakes up."

I could only plead, "My family, they'll leave, they'll leave without me."

Inside, constrained, still sobbing, I went to sit on that rusty, dented cook pot again. I had no other choice; I had to wait for the sleeping man, who had no name other than "commander," to wake up and question me himself.

I spent a few long, absurd hours waiting in that dark, piss-drenched cell, until, really, little by little, I began to feel that the sleeping man, the commander, might be the only hope I had to get set free. I encouraged myself: I thought, "Maybe this 'commander' is a worldly guy with an open mind who knows his soccer. Maybe he'll recognize this sketch is no spy's map to sabotage, but a soccer play. May God have them release me and let me get home to my family, to my mom and dad!"

After a while, my patience thin, I began to look around the room, which was so dark, I could barely see anything. Exploring, I found three old beds. In one, there was a sleeping man, the commander, and in the other two, someone had tossed clothes, belts, and combat boots in a pile. There were also two crooked, wobbly tables. One supported a broken fan. The other held a basket—I thought there might be dates in it since mice darted from it and flies swarmed around it. I thought, "It's weird. They've detained me here since dawn. How did this man not hear all the noise I made? All my complaining and sniffling and sobbing? How did the commander sleep through all that noise?" I sat on the rusty, dented cook pot and contemplated the sleeping man. He'd pulled his blanket up to his mustache and slept silently, completely still, not even snoring, not showing one sign of exhaustion, dreams, or life. My heart began to race. I told myself, "I fear that this man will be even more pig-headed and harsh than the other two policemen. I mean, he's their commander. He may even command this whole desert. A commander is able to do everything and does whatever he wants." I was so scared, scared not only that my mom and dad would leave me and that I might never, ever see them again, but that in the end, the commander would execute me over this pathetic piece of paper. I spent another quarter hour in the grip of this angst and anxiety. In those fifteen minutes, three times I heard the distant, sputtering voice of some vehicle—a voice awfully like those of military transport trucks, a voice both distinct from and mixing with the barking of dogs. Each time, with the sputtering of each truck, I thought, "There goes my family," "That was my mother and father and little sister," "They are displacing them again!" And I had no idea where to, which region, which spit of land.

I was out of patience. I couldn't stand it anymore. Abruptly, again, I stood and opened the door. In the doorway, I looked out: No guard was posted. I crept out, casting my eyes first to one side and then the other: There was no one. The place was absolutely deserted. I threw my gaze into the distance and saw a few camels tethered under a scrub date. The terrible, empty silence of the place enveloped me. I felt fatally alone and foreign. It hit me then that I could run and save myself, but that didn't seem decent or proper: I wanted all of them, even the commander, to assert I had committed no crime and that it was my right to go free. Unwillingly, unconsciously, as if drawn to the commander by a very old, strong friendship, I returned to my prison. I went over to his bed and stood there. I looked him over. Noiselessly, I reached out, grabbed his arm, and shook it. "Commander, sir!"

The commander didn't move.

I shook his arm again and called out, "Commander! Commander!"

Again, he didn't move or respond.

This time, I pulled the blanket off him and lifted his hand up. I let go and it fell back down, lifeless, motionless. That's when I knew the commander was dead.

Seeing the corpse in the hush of that dark room, I almost fainted. I wanted to shriek and scream, but no! I just ran outside.

At the threshold, I was ambushed, surrounded by four policemen, all broad-shouldered, burly, dark men: this side, that side, flustered, confused, their rifles leveled at my chest, each man on a hair trigger. Paralyzed, I still managed to meet their eyes.

And an efendi, with pockmarks, a chin-tattoo, and a blue necktie, emerged from behind the policemen and walked toward me. One of the policemen who'd spoken with me earlier ordered the rest, "Arrest him!"

The efendi, with his blue necktie, torn ear, and deep scar across his forehead, looked like a frenzied pedophile I would see again in my nightmares. He loosed a cruel grin as he slowly approached me. He asked the policeman, "This is him?"

The policeman said, "Yes, this is him."

That's when I heard the sputtering voices of the last military transport, steadily, so steadily, leaving the village, getting farther and farther away. And I, a paralyzed wretch, couldn't even scream . . .

Paris
Winter 1989

The Brand on the Back
of My Hand

HOW STRANGE...

That great joy would bring me to the brink of death. That the sudden comfort of a memory might actually kill me. How can I believe any of this? I never saw it coming: that some empty arak bottle, trashed in some back alley, would hand me resolution that has been so resistant and is now so far-reaching. The lost and elusive answer I've spent years searching for, wrestling with throughout my childhood. How strange ... What triggered this memory? Why would it detonate after all these years? How is the dark cave of all my anguish and aberration abruptly awash with light? How?

Yes, how many times have I come right back here, to this black city bursting with bitter childhood memories, to understand the reasons behind every slurry of spit and slurs, every eviction, every thrashing, every flogging my father gave me, except this brand on the back of my hand; that one reason became a mirage, a far-flung port I could never reach. I couldn't even recall what caused the ugly incident. But now . . . so strange . . . how? Here, lazily, as if in a dream, the pieces drift down and settle onto the blank page of my mind. And it's strange: Until this moment, I've been stuck in my child-hood shame, doubt, and aberration. These three each had a twin: the daily hunger, pain, and exhaustion of my child-hood. All such constant companions. As a child, I survived. As I got older, I felt more and more anguish, more and more aberrational, more and more volatile. Agh . . . how have I let myself live in such pain and misery? Because I was surviving. If only this had happened to another kid . . . but then, still, God; this filthy, bulky brand my hand bears, where did it come from? And what it has done to me! This fetid, maggot-infested wound. It was enough to thoroughly disgust me, so what of other people? When I looked around: the wealthy neighborhood kids, their gold rings and delicate watches shimmered on their hands, and me . . . this filthy, ugly brand on mine. So why? Why? The kid I used to be, what could that kid possibly have done? Even if I had com-mitted some terrible crime, how could my father, in good conscience, judge that I deserved this? How? Why? Was this some punishment for some crime I could not possibly have intended? God, why this brand? When, how, where, why mark me? What did I do? I still have no idea. No, I'm not lying to myself. I've never lied to myself. As a child and then far beyond childhood, all those long years, deep in my gut, I tended to silence, a silence that took root and grew from my own feeling that I was a waste, good for nothing, an aberration. This is my eighteenth autumn, and, lost to this one-person epidemic, I've never experienced the comfort or happiness life has offered every other person my age. My childhood was reduced to facing whatever fights came, keeping my distance from others, and keeping in mind my own inferiority. Acquaintances and friends only meant future black eyes. And after my father's death, anything beautiful or good seemed all the more perverse. This knot, this aberration, deep inside me, day by day, grew and grew, and got harder to untangle. So I avoided the hell that all the beautiful parks, picnic spots, avenues, tennis courts, stadiums, and cafés became. I never showed my face. They so filled me with shame and misery, I flinched away from them. After all, how could I taint others with the yellow-bellied aberration I was? It was a relief when these things would fade into the background of my mind, but whenever my eyes would fall on some roadside ragged, beaten, half-charred kid, the vortex, my own personal hell of doubt, would suck me back in. A thousand times I have wished that this brand had come with acid applied directly to my soul. It would have been better . . . but no . . . I couldn't help it . . . and more than anything, I reconciled myself to isolation. Yes, I never did deserve to sit and talk and laugh among friends, well met, out in public. If I even chanced into a crowd, once again, raw shyness and shame would overwhelm me. And if someone said a word or made some joke with even the slightest relationship to the filth on the back of my hand, I'd yank my puny, weak body back, like a frightened mole, and hold myself, once more, to the familiar paths of anxiety. It's so shameful it's unbearable for a kid to come sit among friends and talk with this bulky, filthy brand on the back of his hand, a mangy scar that he's always fighting to hide with the hem of his threadbare sleeve. And even if he manages to hide that, he cannot hide the even bulkier brand misery has left inside.

Ah, God, thank you for the merciful drunkard who took to the bottle last night to console his heart; and now mine. For years and years, I have struggled with insomnia. I have wept at how shy and inferior I felt around other people. Miserable, desolate, how I cried, I still remember, under those old quilts! So many times, when we'd visit my relatives, or when they'd come to visit my poor mother, I remember so well: how they took such pride in their beauty, jewelry, fancy houses, and all their land, how under the guise of jokes, they'd stone me and the thin glass of my existence. I will never forget that they told my mother, "There isn't a girl on Earth who'd marry your boy!"

Ah, how I clung to our misfortune, which never abandoned us though we were shabby and destitute, though I was a blight. I wanted to say just one word, something to their faces, but knew if I opened my mouth, all that would come out would be accusations and insults. No, I kept my mouth shut. I scoured my heart with my muffled tears, tears that did not give our hunger or sorrow away to those in their palaces and mansions. Anyhow. So, what? It seemed . . . ah, it is strange . . . it seems I'm just now discovering some things. Yes. Sure. There's no question: If I had not been the son of such a poor father, I wouldn't have had to suffer this aberration and its attendant shame. And those people back then couldn't have humiliated and hurt me the way they did. No. Never mind. Leave it be. I learned so much from the battered kid who lives on inside this scarred person.

Never mind . . .

So, what . . .

Let me not turn back, no, to a past full of sorrow, marked by aberration.

I mean . . . I wasn't to blame. How could I have been? No, I have never been to blame. Still today, in this wayward, sinful, cursed city of ours, there are destitute kids who steal or make some other awful mistake and get on the wrong side of the law or are taken in by the brutish men who loiter around movie theaters, rosaries in hand, child-molester mustaches drooping low, and their parents scar their hands or tan their hides for it. I was a poor kid like that and there was nothing I could do. My heart grew heavy and my mind got stuck on all the ways I fell short and stuck out. I etched disgrace and disgust into my imagination, sweating out my humiliation in rivers around my ears; all that water and still, I was no droplet of misery that could trickle away into the soil . . . I consoled myself that at least I had no memory of the event, not even one I could remember letting go of or giving up. So, what was it? This brand on the back of my hand? Agh, it was strange. And this numb forgetfulness made me consider myself quite the absent-minded, even oblivious kid. Every time I asked my beleaguered mother about this, in her irritation and distraction, she'd curse my father, the very person who'd marked me so shamefully. And every time, she'd say, "Why do I still have two words left for that harsh and hot-tempered man?"

Agh, what a cruel man. What a trying and hard-hearted

man. And the gambling just crushed my tiny heart. I haven't thought much about this habit of his . . . Oh, and maybe that caused the pennilessness and hardship that had a stranglehold on our home. I remember the cold, dark nights he'd come home late from the club near our house, busted, hungover, exhausted, gambling and drinking having cleaned out every pocket he had. My mother would duck under the quilts to whisper, as if it were a secret, "Here he is, the high roller, come home again." Then, the high roller would hurl his frustration and anger, like so many stones, at me and my poor mother. And some nights, shouting and swearing, as if in a riot, he'd kick me out of the house and leave me to fend for myself on the dark streets and the cold, forbidding sidewalks. Under a tree or maybe a chair a coffee shop had left out, I'd curl up, a stray, a stranger. This cruel, hard-hearted man, though I was just a kid, took me out of school and put me to work in his shop. And how well I remember that shop. Yeah. Even now, I can see it so clearly: A medium-sized butcher shop, divided in two by a wall with a gap in the middle left open for the frequent traffic. He worked out front, reserving the back exclusively for the evenings; he'd set out glasses of arak and some appetizers and sit with whichever Gypsy woman or plastic bag vendor or prostitute who'd agreed to meet him there; they'd have their eager, sloppy celebration. He turned the back half of the store into his own semiprivate brothel. Agh, and I, when they stole their moments in the back of the store, wrapped up in each other, in a river of naked lust, groaning and moaning, I was left to man the storefront, left to my own hungers and thirsts, so disconsolate, absolutely exhausted. And how I wished, in those moments, even if only for a few brief moments, someone would usher the exhaustion from my body and allow me to rest in my mother's warm and loving arms; if only once I could feel like a child . . .

Ah, God, why can't I get over my childhood hunger, deprivation, and alienation? Ah . . . how I long to be a child once more and see my father come to me and just once hug me and give me a fistful of sweets and small change. How I long to be a child once more, but dressed in clean clothes, not one patch, even if just for a single Eid, and sit to watch a cowboy or Ringo movie . . . maybe . . . I'd sit down and . . . never . . . grow up! But no . . . no . . . all that exists now only in my imagination and nowhere else. Instead of any of that, the man made me his shadow, apart from him only when he'd send me off to do housework or hard labor in some pot-holed and pitted mud patch of a neighborhood or fetch him his lunch or buy him some arak or entertain a friendly prostitute as she waited for him. Only then would I get out from under that man's heavy fists and hateful shadow. Agh, how that human took things from me and perverted their every meaning. When he gave me this brand, he took the meaning of my own existence, the meaning of any satisfaction or fullness or comfort that I glimpsed among my wealthy, well-dressed friends. And how could I fail to ask him while he was alive about what has kept me in knots? This aberration? The questions seemed impossible. I didn't dare ask. Why... ever since I was a child, the man instilled in me such deep terror and trembling, I couldn't imagine even approaching him. That's the way it was, so, what could I have done? I mean, how could I have been anything other than anxious and aberrant? After I'd been stubborn or gone berserk, after I'd wet the bed, after any obvious offense, I knew I'd be punished. Or some days, when I brought him lunch from home, I'd linger at the park fountain, watching kids splash around in it and play marbles around it and I'd get lost in jealousy, marveling at their luck. I'd forget that with every passing minute, dad was only getting hungrier and more rabid and I'd have to bring him his meal late and cold. Or when I'd pinch one or two coins from the till. Or when I'd fight a rich neighbor's kid. All of these times, I knew exactly why I was punished; even now, they come back to me one by one as if they happened yesterday. But the incident behind this brand so stunned and surprised me, I can't remember it. Until this moment, I have been consumed by these questions: What ugly thing must have happened to me? What crime must I have committed? Until this evening, these questions have torn me apart with all their teeth, like so many sharpened daggers. But now . . . the truth is, it's strange . . . how can I believe it? Yet here it is . . . so strange, it's sublime. I'm laughing now. How could I not? How could I not laugh on this of all days?

That day, curse that day, like so many other evenings, my father had met up with one of his women and left the store to me. And I, by late evening, couldn't help it, I was desperate to pee. I couldn't run to the nearby mosque and leave the shop unattended: I knew that if he came back to an empty shop, he would lose his mind and give me an unholy beating. I was too shy and too old to simply pee outside in a crowded market. I was at the end of my rope. Then, I have no idea how, but I found myself on the far side of our store's dividing wall, where he rutted and drank arak. There, at least no one could see me. But soon there, too, I got scared: What would he do to me when he came back if he somehow sensed, through the stench and smear of it, that I'd peed? Out of sheer misery, I peed in one of the warped arak bottles rattling around back there. Suddenly relieved, I forgot all this, even the once-empty arak bottle now filled with pee. Until this fine evening, I didn't know—how could I have known—that later, my father, drunk, would find that same bottle and try to guzzle it down!

Hawler

1979

A New Address

YOUR SKULL, LIKE A CAPITAL CITY, echoes with hollers and horns and a great horde. Your crestfallen reflection only makes you more so. You want to crisscross the city. Shops, mosques, bars, cars, pushcarts, foreigners, madmen, police, jackasses, and weary stragglers clog the sidewalks and streets. Through the fuss and fret and filth and freshness of the late evening, in your threadbare clothes, it's obvious: You are a tenderhearted and strange young man whose father has kicked him out of the house. It's so obvious: You have picked yourself up and turned your back on the cruelty, clacking, and calloused hands of a father. A plastic bag and some books in your hands, as if you have traveled some winding and long road, though calm, your eyes rove; and your heart, like a snowball on a stovetop, melts and yet remains . . .

This late evening, your restlessness digs at your heart. What a lonely, wounded iconoclast you are! If, right now, the whole city—the great and the small, known and unknown, from near and far—came to drown your heart in pitchers of love, to shade your heart with compassion, you'd feel nothing. As ever. You can't. You can't get over your broken, patchwork heart. The dry hurricane that carried you off has made you a stranger to these streets. You are a son of this city; several years away, studying in another city doesn't make you a fool among the homes, alleys, and avenues of your own, neither does it obscure your strangeness or your low spirits. It's strange. You also wonder: Why am I unmoved when my family and friends speak? Conferences and casinos, sprawling lawns and movie theaters, none give me a sense of beauty or joy. Ah, why doesn't the flood of that happiness run through the desert of my heart? I wish I understood my soul's relentless hunger and thirst. But why bother? What can I do? Only my loneliness . . . my loneliness alone tugs the poles of my agony and ecstasy nearer each other.

You light a cigarette. This isn't your first time. You remember how many other times you ran from your cramped and crowded house, from your stunned mother and wasted father, the father you couldn't seem to accept as your father no matter how hard you tried. He constantly spat at you, cursing, raising a fist or a belt, driving you like a stray into the neighborhood's cold, dark alleys. The only peace and comfort in your life was in those moments when the night reached out to stroke your hair with her fingers, when your father, under cover of that darkness, with a few other mustachioed, muscle-bound men, walked over to the nearby café to gamble and drink. You know that man, that king of cowards who hates books. The man who tears up and burns every book you buy and read. The kind of man who makes you love time more than luck. But here it is: This evening, once and for all, you left. You picked yourself up and left, without looking back . . .

You flick your cigarette butt into the street. With unending sadness, you gaze at the crowds and chaos there. Out of nowhere, the horns and screeching of a mess of colorful cars startle you. Beggars, Gypsy women, men selling from pushcarts or right from their pockets slip from the street to the sidewalk. What is all this celebrating and self-forgetfulness as the city grieves and mourns over which of its woes? Silently, something breaks inside you. You raise your shining, sad eyes. You want to find a hotel room as soon as possible; a hotel that will accommodate the pain and pure longing of your youth, a hotel that can hold your plastic bag, smattering of books, and shattered skull. How many hotels are there in this city where the price of sleep isn't one more hobgoblin in your soul? You look around. What do you know? The darkness thickens and pours into the streets, which, little by little, empty of people. And the hotels will mostly likely be overrun with vagabonds, military men, bachelors, smugglers, and asylum seekers. Your heart sinks: Perhaps with all the old country farmers who've come to the city looking for work, with all the Egyptian and Hindu laborers, there won't be any vacancies. You crave another cigarette. You reach into your pocket. Your fingers brush against Zaynab's letter. Like a movie, all the dreams and sorrows of the recent years play across your mind. Her great shadow engulfs you. How you cherish every street, every alley of her city. Now that she's far away, you have only her letters to assuage your anguish and keep you close to her sorrows, desires, and dreams. One sentence from the letter has burrowed into your mind, "The life we build will not have some miserable corner for you or four hateful walls choking me."

You take a deep drag off your cigarette. You climb the hotel stairs. You get your answer. The rate, well, it isn't so bad. You pay through the end of the month. No one needs to help you with your bags. You travel light. You open the door to a small room. You throw your plastic bag and books onto the bed. The mattress and the blanket are much older than your sorrow. The wall and the bed frame are even more exhausted and downtrodden than you are. And with that, right here, you raise the flag of the endless sorrow of your wandering. Curse every father and every father's household! Only here, in this hotel, in this solitary and self-contained room, can you finally listen to your own injuries, memories, and laments. Here, no one will put your griefs or desires or dreams to death, no one—just because he calls himself your father—will impose his ridiculous demands on you, and no one will burn your books. The image of a muscle-bound, mustachioed man, some kind of movie actor, hangs in the center of the wall and grabs your attention. Your severe and sullen father materializes before your eyes. You see again that one evening when your mother expressed pity for her own white hair and the honor of the women her husband bought and your father flew into a rage. "Whether you like it or not," he said, "this is how it is. You're worth less to me than this pair of shoes."

It wasn't so important for you to recall such a scene. Calmly, you study the hotel window. Like every sorrowful, lonely man does in such rooms. The window looks like a painting on the wall, dark and full of distant yellow stars. You approach the window to look down on the street below.

The street, as if someone just brandished a knife, is deserted and still. Distant drunks sing with distant barking dogs.

You go back to your bed. Your mind churns. You take out the notebook. How can you write the stories of millions of starving, displaced, friendless, abandoned people? With the blood of hundreds of untimely deaths and martyrs and murder victims as your pen's ink? Entire lands swallowed up by earthquakes or volcanic eruptions, people of the world hurting, stripped, starving, so hungry their bellies have distended, poor, dark-skinned women trying to nurse and so thirsty their breasts have run dry, children—girls—terrified as napalm suffocates them, entire villages burned . . . how can you . . . how can you write something like that and settle your unsettled heart? Ah, God, how long can a human body weep before it runs dry? You write through the tears. You still write. You break out into a hot sweat. You jump up.

Abruptly, you pick up your pen once more to write to the dark, brimming, yearning eyes of Zaynab: the eyes in which you found all sorrows and dreams, the eyes in which you swam, laughed, cried, and danced. You get a fresh piece of paper to write Zaynab a letter. You write, "Beloved, my dear Zaynab, I've become a stranger in my own city, friendless, lonely, and penniless. Until I find a job, along with some sweet words of yours, please send me some money."

With that, you finish the letter, leaving your new address on the envelope.

1980

Zaynab and More

GET UP!

Come on, get up . . . come . . . get to your feet!

In just a few seconds . . . it'll all be over.

Come on now, don't seize up, no regrets or hesitation; enough idly looking back on the past with its hatred and fury. That's pointless. Get up; wrap up your tears, your sorrows, your wounds and get out!

No one will know a thing until dawn when everyone wakes up. Maybe. No, no one will know. And don't tip anyone off. Let your leaving be unlooked for: a sudden sorrow, even anguish. Come, get up . . . come on!

Ah, and now that this is the last night of your life, you wish with all your heart to take in your cold, unkempt room with one last glance, a glance that contains both your remorse and your farewell. There, when you turn to that side, is Kamiyar, your little brother, in his disheveled bed, sleeping so lightly. The scared slant of his cheek fills you with that much more sorrow and weariness. Agh . . . come, get up; give him the last kiss of his faithful, kind sister and go!

You are quite comfortable, happy even, now that you've chosen this dreadful path; your only concern is tomorrow's. After you go, what to-do will sweep the neighborhood? The women, the girls—what chitchat, what murmurs will they manufacture? Who will whisper in whose ear, "Foolish girl. How could she have done this?"

Then Shawnim and Hassiba will arrive, weeping in front of all those vultures, making a good show of their grief. But no . . . nah . . . those two sisters of yours, when they'd heard the news, they would have nearly died from joy and sheer relief. Yeah, yes, it would be as if they had won a difficult battle without lifting a finger, without even getting their hands dirty; inside, they'd be cackling. Neither would reveal their joy or relief even to the other, but silently their hearts would pump the same joy and relief through their narrow veins. The shame and scandal of your leaving will linger for a few weeks, then fade. When all the noise has died down, perhaps a lucky sprite will grace the house. Perhaps the house could then finally welcome abundant blessings and goodness and happiness. Yes, from then on, they wouldn't miss whatever money fell from their purses. Yes, after you're gone, they'll live so much more comfortably than now, so much more stylishly. No doubt about it, the money for your comings and goings, your overnight trips, the money for your blouses and camisoles and your various makeup kits, your weekend bag, your slippers and bottled perfumes, even your bras . . . it will all go to them, it will all go back to the little box on the rotting windowsill. Finally, their blame and accusations will dissipate. From then on, they'll spend the rest of their lives, all their days, in a comfortable and peaceful house: not another night seeing you—exhausted, depleted, and disgusted—come home and throw your purse on the bed, the traces of some entitled man's scent and kisses still on your mouth, breasts, and neck, confusing them and leaving them somehow heavyhearted. Yes, not another morning of their envy and hatred. Not one more time will they see you stand in front of the mirror in some dress, tidying your hair, running your hands over your face where smallpox left its dirty marks and crows their footprints. Not one more time will they see you turn and walk away with indifferent steps to your obligations, closing the back door on them. Not one more time will they see you, later, as you come back, so many johns, some in ties, trailing you home.

It's over. It's over. No more. From now on, their snide chitchat and whispers will dissipate into the night. But it's strange: How is it that tonight they've fallen silent? They never are. You think they have somehow guessed at this desperate plan of yours? It can't be. So what is this silence tonight? What are they doing now, in this dreadful silence? Maybe just sitting around. Yeah, could be. They're just sitting around. For a while now, every night, until one in the morning, they drowse fitfully, they can't sink into sleep; they just toss and turn, on one flank and then the other; when they get completely irritated and exhausted, they flop on their backs like two tired, wounded pigeons and gaze at the soot-blackened rafters, jutting out like ribs from the room's cramped and grimy roof; without a sound, without a flame, they burn in their own private hell. They burn and don't even get to die. Oh, these two sisters of yours were not always like this. No, they never were. The cheerfulness and games and jokes and pillow fights they used to have: Where have they gone? Where are they now? No. Yeah, you have known them well. Agh, though for so many months you've stewed in their hatred, you haven't snapped. Yes, now whenever you ask them to come with you to the bazaar, or to visit family, they trail after you with none of the enthusiasm they used to have; they find excuses like they're ill or worn out, anything to split off from you. They used to bring their knitting needles and skeins and embroidery thread to the stoop and woolgather with the neighborhood women late into the night, chewing gum and chatting while stitching hats and sifting bulgur. Not anymore. Now, as if terrified by some spiteful spirit outside, they slam the door as soon as the sun sets; subdued by the humiliation and shame they feel, they creep back to their cramped and dingy room. No, these aren't the same sisters you've known. Their eyes don't shine with clarity and depth, but hide fiery hate or doubt. No. These are not the eyes in which you found refuge and joy. No. You never see those eyes anymore. Behind every smile lies a great burden: sorrow, suffering, and regret. With your own ears, you've heard them accuse, blame, and dig at you. Yeah, even now, here they are—through the wall—you can hear them. Yes, of course you hear them whispering and making fun. Yeah, here they are, talking about you, always the same script of blame and jabs. And, of course, the words must be said through tears, even sobs. Nah. Yeah, Shawnim is a dreadful crybaby. There, that's her weeping and wailing that's sinking into your ears like the most grievous graveside melody. But Hassiba is more grown up. She doesn't cry like that; she sticks to herself for comfort. And her insides are full, full of hate, remorse, and reproach. This one—like a river foaming and roaring with frenetic, lethal waves—she's a scraper: This one drowns even the waves with her sorrowful silence. When will she explode? Explode and sweep away everything in her path like Noah's cursed flood. When? Why not? Of course, that's within her reach. What she had done this evening was nothing compared to . . . no . . . ah. How you wish you'd never seen yourself this way. Well . . . leave it be. After all, she's right. It isn't right. Yes. You're her eldest sister and know every detail, all the nitty-gritty: She had taken up with the son of Mawlood, the lame gardener. Then, the other day, without your knowledge, she confided in your neighbor, Aunty Haibat, in the hopes that she would tell the boy's family who would come make a proposal and that would be that. Instead, lame, trite Mawlood visited having already decided, "Let's leave it once and for all. There's nothing left to say."

Then, he turned around and told all the neighbors, "We want nothing to do with this girl, a prostitute's sister; the whole neighborhood knows the infamous Zaynab."

They even threw in that her sisters now hide behind the pretense of selling eggs to stay at Sharif Agha's house every night until two in the morning. And that's that . . . other than, what else did some spinster whore expect from such a murky, sloppy city? What do people have to say about her except damning and backbiting? And it's strange: After all is said and done, you—you on your own, that's fine: But these sisters of yours? You don't understand. What sin did they commit? Why must isolation and humiliation leach all color from their hair, while they sit, shame-faced and neck-deep in this black morass? No, no, it's a shame! You will never commit this sin: You will not forgive yourself; you will live with all your sins until you draw your last breath. No, there isn't a single teardrop left in your being to shed over the future's sins and sorrows. You are now a soul void of tears. You can't sidestep their hangdog misery anymore. Nah and agh, it took you too long to notice this hell of theirs; well and done, it can all end in just a few more moments. Come on, get up! No; sigh no sighs of blame or rebuke; don't consider Hassiba stonehearted, disloyal, or ungrateful. No. The memory of how she fought and screeched this evening, erase it from your mind at once. It's Hassiba's right, and very much so. You know: Having a husband is everything to them. Yeah, that's it. It seems you, you, the spinster passing through rotting houses, must always have a man to tell you that you are comfortable; always have a man to tell you that you exist. Agh, but then why was there no man for you; except for filthy, greedy wolves, why was there no man for you? Agh. Leave it. Let it be . . .

Your breath is a sigh of grief.

Your life, a morose and meandering stream, has flowed past! The moment Dad left this world your comfortable, happy nest fell apart. Only now, now that you think about it, only now do you realize what tremendous shade and shelter that man gave you! Back in those days, your neighbors, Aunty Zibed and Aunty Safiat, their daughters had to sell paper bags in the market and peddle syrup on the sly; but Dad . . . your father saw this as shameful, even humiliating: He didn't allow his daughters to do more than make hats and embroider; so long as he lived, he provided for you all with his own sweat. But he left . . . not to return. Mom, ill and grieving, left you not long after. What could you do? You existed . . . and when you exist, you're forced to find some way to survive. You were the eldest, and, more than any, you felt keenly that high cost and deep harm. You forbid Shawnim from quitting school as she said she would, and Hassiba? You made sure she busied herself only with tailoring, crocheting, and adorning shawls and scarves for the women of the neighborhood. You made yourself face the job in the factory, an ill-fated factory and your bad luck, a factory that your two sisters, even now, fail to understand as the place of duplicity, depravity, and oppression that it is. Agh. A thousand times agh: From the outside, the walls were so colorful.

You had no idea what wolves and beasts lurked within. You were a provincial girl who was suddenly a seamstress inside four rotting, sallow walls. You didn't know. Agh. If you had known, you would have drowned any kindness, any hunger, any desire within you, like a fawn, desperate for water, even from a great distance, you would have scented and avoided man and his bright cars; you'd have left them alone with their sated stomachs and insatiable hunger! So what? Agh, you're sorry now. So very sorry. Dilshad was a tricky bastard: Whenever he got lucky, after, he'd crumple money into your clutches and say, "I can't wait to marry you." He was the one who introduced you to Shakir, the goldsmith, and Shawkat, the shopkeeper: Shawkat who knew nothing more of loyalty, kindness, and love than the value of gold, money, and lust. It's all pointless . . . all just gone. Now even the most brainless, the most brutish of men, wouldn't have you. Agh, who would believe that your firm body and beautiful face would have gone slack this early? Who would believe that even once you'd break your sisters' hearts? But today, here it is: You're hell on them. Still, it's good they will remain. Here, then, are the last tears you have in your being and you shed them for your sisters. But no, don't weep! Enough consuming grief, enough pain over this evening's fuss. No, don't weep; it's simply not necessary. After you, they won't have any more cause for shame, misery, or pain. People will even respect them. Then, once every three months, they will go collect the pension and split it. The family won't have to waste their money anymore on your shit. Yes, then when they get married, they will be addressed as Lady and Miss. Yes . . . come, get up, come on!

Come on. Enough looking back on the hatred and fury of the past! Enough vomiting up your sins and memories. Get up. Come on. There: The knife in the saucepan is so close. Pick it up! It'll all take less than a few seconds and . . . done. You'll be on your way to the last comfort, the last home in your life. You seized the knife with trembling hands. Like a deer, trussed up and terrified, in the hands of death, you heaved and panted. Sobs bubbled up and the tears boiled out and the racket of some strange, exhausted creature permeated your room, startling the stillness. Through your clear and ebbing tears, you gazed at the mirror hanging midwall: your hands with the knife trembling. Before you drove the knife into your heart, you saw your pitch-black blood spilling in the mirror. Before you howled at the pain of your departure, you heard yourself scream, scream and groan hideously like a madman. Your little brother, Kamiyar, who had been curled up like a cat, asleep in his bed just beside you, startled up, shocked and staring at you, his mouth hanging open. The knife fell from your hands. You knelt down to Kamiyar. Your eyes brimming with tears, your soul brimming with kindness and longing and the unknown, you buried his eyes, brimming with surprise and curiosity and questions in your embrace . . .

1981

The Wild Windflowers of Kotal

WHEN I WOULD RING THE BELL, she would always come to the door for me. I would listen and feel from far off a butterfly, settling into the courtyard: the soft scuff of her footsteps, the rustle of her dress against the courtyard, laid in fragrant stone, lush on both sides with greenery, restoring my psyche. I always had to gather my courage to say to her, "Good evening, Shadan."

"Good evening."

Standing on that threshold, I managed a shy smile.

She'd say, "Come in."

The door behind us, she'd lead the way. In their brief courtyard, not out of shame, but to make sure, I'd pretend to look at the basil or at the yellow and red flowers edging the greenery. In a whisper, I'd ask her, "Who's here?"

And without turning to me, she would whisper, even more skittish than I, "No one, just my mother."

That was her customary answer. Then, without hesitation, without shame, we would climb the few stairs and enter through the hallway's double doors.

Ah, but this time she won't know that it's me knocking on the door, she won't know who, really who, is knocking on her door this evening so out of time! She'd never expect me.

Perhaps now, as most evenings in the old days, she's sitting in a corner of her room, or, as she used to sometimes, on the lawn, in the green rocking chair, in her thin-hemmed dress, reading a book, so exhausted and sorrowful she might not even care that someone rang the bell, she might even let her mother or her sister Su'ad come to open the door.

Miss Su'ad, her older sister. I think she was seven, yes, seven years older than Shadan. Agh, that hapless, disgraceful evening! I'm still mortified. But we never saw it coming! On the pretext of studying, we had retreated to an upstairs room: She came over to me, placed both hands firmly on my neck, pulled my head to her breast, straddled my legs, and sat down on my lap; suddenly, the doorknob rattled and we sprang apart, but Miss Su'ad had seen us. She blushed, shut her eyes tight, said nothing, and hastily closed the door on us.

From that day on, if I knew Miss Su'ad was at home, I wouldn't go, even for the shortest of visits; and if I happened to be at their home when Miss Su'ad came home, I couldn't face her at all, I couldn't even raise my eyes to meet hers.

Will Miss Su'ad answer the door for me this time? It would be so strange! I'm sure: Even after all this time and all these long days, the scene of that evening—like the fading, echoing peals from a church belfry in a distant village—resounds in her mind. And it's possible, too, that seeing me, she won't believe her eyes, that it will seem beyond strange to her that after all these years, after so many days, I would appear like a ghost or an angel to ring their doorbell and say, "Good evening, Miss Su'ad!" It is strange. I feel so uncertain. Throughout these long years, in all the letters Shadan sent me, she never included any news of her sister. In her letters, she never mentioned, "Su'ad got married!" She did always say, "My older sister will never marry," and, "After her fiancée was arrested and executed, she couldn't see anything in the world but darkness."

Come on, don't do this to yourself. Only a few more moments, only a few more minutes, and I'll be at their door. Then I can ask her myself for news of Miss Su'ad, Trifa, Aso, and of her brothers, one by one, and of her cousins . . . news of everyone, news of Chinoor, Pakhshan, and of all her close friends who were our classmates at university: those who envied our pure, iridescent love and those who adored us. Agh, a thousand times I've wished to go back to those school years. What a dream. Such a sweet dream! Every evening, when classes were over, we grieved that we had to part from one another; profound sorrow and dread overtook us, but no, the night would not fall so early: We still had a few more hours under the sun, a few more bright hours of walking through the streets. As a couple, we would begin walking, deep in pleasant conversation, from the university toward the narrow alley near Halkawt High School until we reached the intersection with Tui Malik Street. And from there, our surroundings became more colorful, the air sweeter, the world more beautiful. As we walked the long street of Ibrahim Pasha, our steps would get slower and slower. One day, I remember, we had stopped on a corner. Standing there, she smiled at me and said, "I'd love it if this street were longer!"

"Why?" I asked.

"So our walks could be longer," she said.

As we arrived at the end of Ibrahim Pasha Street, the cemetery spread out before us. We stood in the alley next to the ice factory for a moment more: Thinly veiled sorrow settled over our faces, as if each time we said goodbye would be the last. In the end, when she walked away, I stood still just to watch her from behind: Her hips swayed so sweetly as she climbed the hill to their street. Before she reached the fourth door, on the right-hand side, several leafy branches and sprigs had managed to hang their slight necks over a leaning, leaking cinder block wall. At the threshold, she would throw me one last glance and duck inside.

Ah, you think these scenes will last . . . then, only moments later, minutes later, they end. Here, here again, after five years of wandering, fleeing, and carrying my only home on my back, Ibrahim Pasha and the ice factory materialize once more before me . . . right here!

By God, and I was a fool and a coward! She's right to think me disloyal. The truth of it is that only once, only once in these last five years—and then only frantic and pressed— was I able to set foot in their neighborhood. It was late one cold, snow-driven night. I remember. I had a bunch of declarations and manifestos with me, as well as three or four letters Shahab, "The Nose," had written for his mother. I was supposed to paste the declarations and manifestos onto the walls along Ibrahim Pasha Street and deliver the letters to Shahab's house in Sabunkaran. I could barely keep myself together. I remember, even at Shahab's house, I couldn't sit still to share a cup of bitter tea with the family; I darted out to join my comrades, my fellow peshmerga, in Majid Beg, beside Nali's Hamam, where it seemed quieter and emptier than Sera Square, so we could gather and go on to Miss Zuleikha's house, where we prepared ourselves to storm Amna Suraka at one thirty in the morning.

But I don't need to tell a rabbit about the lion and the fox. She's right. In a letter, she wrote, "I know that you've slipped into the city twice and neither time did you think to visit me at home or even call me from a corner payphone. I would have loved just to hear your voice." She's right: Whatever gripes or grievances she has against me, she's right. Whatever else, it's been two years since I've been able to write to her. Two years fleeing, fleeing from this mountain to that mountain, then finally seeking exile on the Iranian side of the border. All this pushed my own name, not just her, out of my head. And, agh, what should I have done?

I'm sure that Shadan is unaware that for the last two years, I've been far from the mountains of Slemani: Government forces closed in on our battalion with planes, bombs, and chemical weapons, chasing us up the peaks and into the valleys of Badinan. She's unaware that I've been wounded twice in the course of the recent bombardments and firefights. She's unaware what pain and torture and hellish impossibilities I've experienced; how, from one village to the next, from one mountain to another, crisscrossing Kurdistan, always, in every minute, every second, I've cried out for her, only her name on my lips! Agh, she's unaware. And how could she know? Agh, it's so strange! We are in our own country, no ocean, no border between us, and still we can't, we just can't see one another . . . not even letters can reliably carry our voices to each other! What hell is this?

But those demanding days are over. And now, here it is: I've come back, I'm in Slemani again! Here I am, on this silent, deserted street, without a single bag, without anywhere to go, without anyone to turn to, utterly alone, like some footloose foreigner visiting a city for the first time, knowing not a soul in an unknown city. I have only a handful of wild windflowers, the ones that Shadan was always crazy about. She used to tell me, "Whenever I see wild windflowers, I always remember our day trip in Kotal."

"Yes, and when was that?"

"The day we first kissed each other."

"I know! But which month was that?"

"I think it was during our fourth year at university."

"It was a Friday evening."

Our whole class packed in with some of our teachers for our spring trip to visit Kotal: Kotal lush with all its streams and mountains, Kotal draped in wild windflowers, bright

sun, and such green. In the evening, after dancing and singing, after eating and drinking till we were full, every couple, each boy and girl, drifted away toward the trees. As we
walked, Shadan and I turned toward a nearby creek. When
we reached the creekbank, I paused and knelt in the midst of
all that green to pick a handful of windflowers, then face her
with a trembling heart.

Shadan gazed at the windflowers in my hands so shyly,
with such warmth and passion, as if I had gathered up my
very soul, my entire existence in that handful. I had to contain
myself; a little shy, but with a voice strengthened by passion,
I told her, "I picked these windflowers for you, Shadan . . . "

I hadn't even held her yet, but she laughed and threw her
arms around my neck, saying, "My love!"

And from that day on, Shadan was in love with wild
windflowers. Whenever we went on one of those trips, or
took a walk, we wouldn't come home without picking a
handful of windflowers. Ah, it's been so many years since we
picked windflowers together. It's been many years since we
buried our noses in windflowers, side by side. But no, this is
it . . . just a few more minutes and that's that! As soon as she
sees these wild windflowers in my hands, she'll light up and
the bitter, awful hardship of these last few years may even
begin to fade in her mind. And then, I know it, the memory

of that last night, that last time, that last farewell, when she walked me out, will rush in: Her eyes swam with heavy, clear tears as she said, "Go, and don't look back."

I said, "I'm scared."

She said, "Of what?"

I said, "That we won't see each other again."

She said, "Rest easy, one more year and I'll graduate. Then I'll be on my way to the mountains!"

But here it is! Ibrahim Pasha Street! The street where we always met and walked and laughed. It's strange. So strange: Has anything changed around here? It's just as it's always been! If I turn where I stand, I can see the hospital that made sure hungry children always had milk; we all still call it "Milk Hospital." And there's the teahouse. I always called their house from that teahouse. Yes, what was their telephone number? Two, one, zero, four . . . but no, I won't call them. That way, my abrupt return will be the kind of unforeseeable surprise that makes everyone giddy. That way, certainly, anyone who answers the door for me will be stunned. They might not even recognize me at first. But, oh, how lovely it will be to step inside, to just walk into their sitting room! And how fun! It'll be a riot! Someone will say, "You've lost weight!" And another will say, "No, he's bulked up." I'm sure that while I'm still just in their courtyard, every one of her little brothers, every one of her sisters, her mother, her father . . . will surround me, peppering me with questions. And in that moment, in all my own confusion and giddiness, I might get tongue-tied and be able only to laugh, not speak. After all, where would I even begin? What could I possibly say? I'll have to cut it short: "I've come under heavy scrutiny. All last night and today, I've been in interrogations, interrogated. They just released me. I came straight to you. I have no family but you!" Then Shadan's parents will understand and I won't have to say anything more.

But I won't show them how burned out I am from the last few years of life as a peshmerga, how sick and tired I am of it all, I won't tell them that I've lost my courage, even lost my faith in all peshmerga. I won't tell them that I lost my faith in Kurdish political parties and so surrendered myself to Saddam's soldiers, no, I won't even mention to them that I was exposed to chemical gas and along with hundreds of other peshmerga and thousands of other wounded. I was removed to a hospital in Tehran and laid up there, injured and ill, for three months; and after that I spent four full months living as a refugee, without a cent, without a soul, without hope, suffering and struggling in Semnan Camp. No. I won't talk about these things in front of her mom and dad and brothers. I'll just say, "It was only a small shrapnel wound that I sustained during the fight for Badinan, in my left shoulder, and that was that. So now that I can't take up arms, I've come home."

Yeah, anyway, that's what I'll say. I don't need to say more and draw it out. Even if they ask after my family, my parents, it's not like they're unaware of the situation in Halabja, it's not like they don't know what's going on. I will not tell them that my entire family, from the youngest to the eldest, got caught in the chemical attack and . . . died. No. I refuse to suddenly shatter these precious few happy moments of pure comfort and overwhelm them with crushing grief and mourning. No! If they ask about my family, I will simply say, "They're doing well. They're in Hamadan, staying with a relative of my father's."

I wiped away my tears and took my finger off the doorbell. It echoed in the courtyard. It didn't take long, as I listened, for the regular beat of footsteps, calm and self-contained, to reach my ears. But it was strange, the footsteps didn't sound human. Whatever it was got closer. Whatever it was had reached the far side of the door.

As I pulled myself together, I noticed that the door had opened, just a crack, all by itself. Then, it gave an abrupt, sheer, short creak and, little by little, swung wide open. No one was there. I got scared.

When I glanced down, a cat was peeking outside. One eye was completely blind and the other was a festering, weeping lump of pus and blood. I winced. I got even more scared. With my right hand, I shoved the door in and bolted up the stairs. No thought, no hesitation: I stumbled inside. In the courtyard, I saw an old woman, hair gone white, hand braced on a crooked stick, coming toward me.

The old woman was clothed head to toe in black, faded, crusted vomit and soup stained her skirt.

When I took in the old woman's features—her mouth, her lips, I felt like some years ago, in some other context, or in a dream, I had seen her, but in my confusion and panic, my mind beyond agitated: I couldn't place her.

The old woman, in the dead center of the courtyard, jerked to a standstill. She rapped her crooked stick against my chest and, chittering like an owl, said something that I couldn't understand; still, it made my soul shiver. I was terrified. I retreated a step.

I stood, stunned, in the courtyard. The old woman, in the same manner, but more flustered, more furious, repeated herself. It dawned on me: She was a mute.

From the threshold, where I stood, determined, I could see inside: On the lawn, a swing hung unevenly from a long, rusty chain. Casually, so casually, it creaked and cracked: a single, sorrowful crack giving rise to a whole ridgeline. Opposite the swing, filthy white sludge, swarmed by flies and midges, drooled down the side of a big, black cookpot for porridge.

My mind was near the breaking point. But still I needed to ask the old woman about Shadan. But at that moment—I don't know what it was—I felt so flustered in front of that old woman, I couldn't even speak Shadan's name. I was reduced to gestures as I asked after Shadan's father. She answered, holding her ground, blustering and making a bit of a bedlam, shaking her crooked stick a time or two toward the sky. She wanted me to understand and I wanted to understand; we couldn't. I wanted her to understand and she wanted to understand; we couldn't. As hard as I tried, as much as I let go, I couldn't coax my voice out of my throat to say, "Shadan! Where is Shadan?"

Suddenly, again, she shoved her crooked stick in my face. Like an epileptic, she foamed at the mouth, trying to articulate something with pain and difficulty that I just couldn't understand. Then, as if weeping, she sobbed out, "Rrrragh . . . ! Rrragh!"

Stunned, I stared at her. And she frowned back, fierce and furious; her crooked stick, once again, gestured and threatened, beating against my chest. As she drove me back, she shrieked, "Rrrrragh . . . ! Rrrragh!"

I was almost mad with fear. From the threshold, I backed up, retreating. My feet tripped me up and I fell onto the stone bench beside the gate. Dazed and downcast, I watched as she raised her crooked stick for the last time and brought it down on me, driving me out, jeering and shrieking at me, "Rrrragh!"

She slammed the door in my face. Driven out, standing in front of that cold door, my heart was near breaking. I couldn't cry. With a disconsolate heart and a wounded soul, I laid the wild windflowers on the stone bench beside the gate; I couldn't bear to see anything more, I just backed up, slowly, retreating . . .

Paris
1988

A Woman

THE BAR WAS CRAMPED, DIM AND DARK, the ceiling blackened like the shadowy heights of an old cave I had seen once in a dream. The walls, gray with dirt and thick with the inescapable stench and smear of vomit, snot, and the sludge the bar served, were interrupted by a few arched windows, rotting and cracking off their frames, with a little paint slapped around. The small hanging lamps over each table splashed dim blue light in slow waves onto each crestfallen face.

The light couldn't cut through the layers of cigarette smoke or brighten the darkness, but each face was still clearly visible. Day laborers, drivers, students, hooligans, retired gentlemen: As I meditated on their faces, I could discern the remnants of the day's grief, dust, and fatigue. And their eyes, clear and glittering, stared out unblinking, shining with an intricate boredom that the darkness could never quite hide. It was strange . . . what was it: this torment, this roving sorrow that always gripped them? They sat as soon as they walked in, like flowers that wither and drop their petals before the tornado's first breath. It was as if they had always known about mourning and lamentation, as if, when they sat, regret and fury and longing could crowd in on their faces. And sometimes, suddenly, as someone left, having slaked his thirst, but not his remorse, he would smash his glass over his own head. Many evenings devolved into fights, chaos, and uproar.

If my friends from my old city were here, they might point out that this noisy dive bar isn't the kind of place a fully employed man like me should frequent every night, all night; but for some reason, ever since I found myself a stranger in this new city, only in this bar could I relax, could I truly breathe. Even now, strangely enough, perhaps it's the love and affection I shared with my dear friend that draws me back, that makes me eager as a lover to visit his old haunt.

This evening, like I've done so many times, with the same old thirst and spirit, I slipped into the bar and sat down. With my same habitual silence, the silence of any single man whose work has taken him to a new, crowded city,

I began to notice and consider the others seated along the bar or at the tables. But, agh, once again, in the absence of my old friend, there was no one to raise his hand in greeting, no one to welcome me, to interrupt how strange and shy I felt; there was no one like him to even offer me a cigarette and ease how lonely and friendless I felt. No one. Among the patrons, I alone felt miserable, friendless, and strange. Still, I couldn't stop looking around. My eyes wandered among the faces, searching for a trace of my friend and his affection; God, let me lay eyes on him again, let him sit beside me a while; let him lighten this burdensome misery, sorrow, and strangeness!

This evening, when I went to sit, when I was barely seated, my gaze fell on a man: a young man, perhaps middle-aged, his coat patched and dirty beyond recognition. It hung from him like the remnants of lengthy torture or some pain or hurt his soul had sustained. Across the room, alone and dejected, he propped his elbow on the table and leaned his head into his hand. A massive and unsightly scar, textured like a healing burn, ran from his temple down to his neck. The scar instantly reminded me of a wound I'd seen on another man's back nineteen years ago as a child in our village; everyone whispered that an eagle had gouged and scarred him so.

I hesitated at first, wondering if this could be my affectionate friend, but as I inspected him more closely, I felt completely certain that this man was indeed the same affectionate friend I'd met here, with all his elegance and grace, so many times before. Truly, my friend had changed quite a bit: restless, indifferent, exhausted. His hair, which had always been so neatly combed, was now a mess, untended and unkempt. Where he'd always been so clean, downright becoming, he now stank of rancid vomit. Leftover okra stew clung to his beard and shirt-collar. Flies hovered around him, buzzing and swarming. Before he came here, my friend must have been deep in his cups at another bar. He was absolutely wasted. He stumbled around his table. He couldn't even lift a hand to shoo the flies away from himself.

When had it been? When had I last seen my friend here? Yes, it was a cold, dusty yellow evening. That evening, the first hazy wisps of winter clouds drifted through the sky, which was choked with dirt and grit as if it hadn't seen even a shower in years. Then, gently, it began to rain. And inside, from my side of the window, I peered out at the street, blurring quickly between the drops: Five or six military trucks and troop transport vehicles drove down the road, one after the other, the rain gradually washing them clean. And, caught by the rain, too, were passersby: some with umbrellas, some without, some alone, some in pairs, all rushed off the street, along the sidewalks, seeking shelter. I said to myself, "When it rains, soggy, humble passersby who might not otherwise crawl into bars." Not long after, a few passersby stumbled in, my friend among them, with his same deliberate and dignified step, defining words like majesty and virility, with the shining countenance, full of affection and sincerity, I had always known; he walked over to a chair at a table surrounded by friends and sat. As always, his friends, as they were accustomed to do, stood as he approached, paying him the respect he deserved, welcoming him warmly, and offering him a cigarette. Then, they called out for another round of arak and picked up their conversation.

Sadly, after that, the man never returned to the bar. And I had been so happy to count him, among everyone in this whole city, as a friend, as he had just begun to turn to my table from time to time so that we could talk with each other. And the truth is, only in his absence did I feel my own fragility: How alone, dismal, and dejected I was each evening in this strange city. And at the same time, I realized how deserted, how dour, and how disconsolate this city, all on its own, was. But still I, feeling keenly alone and alienated for months on end, held out for him. Every night, riddled with anxiety and unslakable thirst, as if I were waiting on the dearest person in my life, I'd sit at my table, staring at the bar's front door.

This evening, when I saw my friend, always so majestic, elegant, and free, now so miserable, abandoned, and broken, I couldn't believe my own eyes. It was strange: The bar was the same bar as before, his friends the same friends as before; so, why was he sitting this time so discouraged and down-cast? Why did his friends, as if he disgusted them, flinch from him? Did they now view every farce they had shared with such distaste and disdain? Why? It was strange! This gentleman's eyes, so pure and clear, used to shine, and now that they are sunk so deep in sorrow, they could never be mistaken for the eyes that once reflected such pride and hap-piness. They are the eyes of a man cornered and humiliated.

Agh, I don't think I'll be able to face this bar ever again, not after tonight. No matter the point or place, if I chance to see this good and affectionate friend of mine again, reduced so, a profound agony will grip me, and my heart will crack wide open.

1982

TRANSLATORS' NOTE

As we began discussing this translators' note, Jiyar said, "Let's leave it. Explaining our process is a kind of interference. We had better leave the reader alone to read. The reading comes first. Open the book. Simply that."

As Jiyar finished his sentence, I felt the simplicity. I saw myself, having found space to read, sit down in a chair with *The Potato Eaters*. I saw myself open the cover. I saw myself begin "The Margins of Europe." That would have been a beautiful way to read this book, to learn Pirbal, to see again how a single human experience, when described well, helps us reach our most intimate and opaque ideas: exile and longing, humor and home, aesthetics and abuse, the desire to be relevant and the refusal to be reduced to relevance. But that is not the way I read this book.

I caught this book in glimpses and through collaboration with others. In 2017, Shook arrived in Iraq as the most recent Artist in Residence at Kashkul, the Center for Arts and Culture that I founded and direct at the American University of Iraq, Sulaimani (AUIS). In 2019, Jiyar Homer began to collaborate with Kashkul. That year, "The Potato Eaters" was among the many poems and stories Shook and Jiyar cotranslated; I gave the English its final edit before Shook quoted from it for their Poetry Foundation essay "A Poet Among Potato Eaters: An Introduction to Farhad Pirbal."

The story itself felt brilliant to me. Sly, dark humor. The perfect confusion of the individual. The glistening heartbreak I knew from classical Kurdish poetry crashing into every reality of Kurdish history in the last couple decades. I wanted to know more. And that's where translation has always begun for me. Jiyar and I agreed to translate *The Potato Eaters* together, while Shook continued translating Pirbal's poetry with Pshtiwan Kamal Babakir, one of my first students when I arrived at AUIS and one of Kashkul's first full-time employees. The process of translating what is now the first collection of Kurdish short stories in English-language publication took four years. Our collaboration grew not from what we lacked, but from how we hoped to challenge each other in service of Pirbal's text.

Some texts invite cotranslation so strongly, it seems like a command. Clare Sullivan, professor of Spanish at the University of Louisville and a talented collaborative translator, edited a special issue of Translation Review focused on translation as community. Community around translation was "a simple fact," she wrote. Forrest Gander, in the article he contributed to the issue, described the Siri Bhoovalaya, a literary work written by Kumudendu Muni, a Jain monk, of over six hundred thousand verses containing at least eighteen scripts coded into Kannada numerals arranged in matrices of 729 squares. Gander did not need to argue for cotranslation: his thorough description of the text did it for him. Perhaps every text is more like the Siri Bhoovalaya than we acknowledge.

But for all its complexities, *The Potato Eaters* is the kind of text that a single translator could approach. And, as translators, Jiyar and I could not be more different. Until *The Potato Eaters*, I had primarily translated poetry, while Jiyar had lived in prose. Perhaps because of my immersion in poetry, I had fierce loyalty to the images, often drawn from the body, that Kurds build their language from. Perhaps predisposed by his immersion in prose, Jiyar chased the immediate legibility and colloquial feel of English. We often argued. We also imagined that the tension between our approaches could well serve an author like Farhad Pirbal, defined by the various tensions he either maintains or explodes with.

The process of cotranslating required persistence. We did not move on from a single disagreement in the translation until we had fully described it and understood where and why we differed. At times, we grew impatient and would "translation fight," as Jiyar called it. Like the narrator and the mute woman in "The Wild Windflowers of Kotal," we would sometimes repeat ourselves, not knowing how to move the conversation forward, but certain we wanted to understand each other. Sometimes we would walk away from a decision, marking our place, knowing that the conversation that day wouldn't budge. That is the nature of understanding: it does not arrive on schedule. We court it. We create conditions for it. We desire it. We do not command it. It just wanders into the courtyard one day, like Pirbal's "Lion," mangy and broken and unbelievable. If we think we can perfect understanding, it teaches us. There is no perfection. There is only paying attention.

That is what Jiyar and I have done. We have paid attention to each other, to Pirbal, and to this book. As readers. As translators. As people. This sounds simple. Simple as leaving someone alone to read. Simple as letting the reading come first. Simple as opening the book.

Alana Marie Levinson-LaBrosse

Newt Beach, California

Acknowledgments

The publisher and translators wish to thank Stephen Beachy and Keith Powell at Your Impossible Voice for bringing "The Lion" to their readers. We would also like to thank the editorial team behind Best Literary Translations (Deep Vellum, 2024). We were honored that Jane Hirschfield, this year's guest editor, alongside co-editors Noh Anothai, Wendy Call, Öykü Tekten, and Kọ́lá Túbọ̀sún, chose Pirbal's "The Lion" for inclusion in the inaugural anthology.

We also want to acknowledge the American University of Iraq, Sulaimani (AUIS) and Kashkul, its Center for Arts and Culture, for bringing us together as colleagues and cotranslators and providing the space to confront work of this magnitude.

A special thank you to Shook for their initial cotranslation of the title story, "The Potato Eaters," and to the Poetry Foundation for publishing Shook's groundbreaking essay, "A Poet Among Potato Eaters: An Introduction to Farhad Pirbal."

Farhad Pirbal (1961–) is an iconic Kurdish writer, poet, painter, critic, singer, and scholar who has lived in Kurdistan, Iraq, Iran, Syria, Germany, Denmark, and France, where he obtained his Ph.D. in history of contemporary Kurdish literature at the Sorbonne. Publishing since 1979, Pirbal has authored more than seventy books of writing, and translation and serves as one of Kurdistan's farthest-reaching voices. In 1994, he founded the Sharafkhan Bidlisi Cultural Center in Hawler. In 2024, marking his English-language debut, Deep Vellum will publish his collected poems, *Refugee Number 33,333*, and his debut short story collection, *The Potato Eaters*.

Jiyar Homer is a translator and editor from Kurdistan, a member of Kashkul, the Center for Arts and Culture at the American University of Iraq, Sulaimani (AUIS), and an editor at Îlyan magazine and the Balinde Poetry publishing house. He speaks Kurdish, English, Spanish, Portuguese, Arabic, and Persian. He specializes in translating Latin American literature into Kurdish and Kurdish literature into various languages, bringing over one hundred authors into publication in more than thirty countries. His book-length translations include works by Juan Carlos Onetti, Carlos Ruiz Zafón, Farhad Pirbal, Bachtyar Ali, and Sherzad Hassan. Additionally, he is a member of Kurdish PEN.

Alana Marie Levinson-LaBrosse is a poet, translator, and professor. She holds a Ph.D. in Kurdish Studies from the University of Exeter. Her book-length works include Kajal Ahmed's *Handful of Salt* (2016), Abdulla Pashew's *Dictionary of Midnight* (2019), and *Something Missing From This World: An Anthology of Contemporary Êzîdî Poetry* (2024). Her writing has appeared in *Modern Poetry in Translation*, *World Literature Today*, *Plume*, *Epiphany*, *The Iowa Review*, and *Words Without Borders*. She serves as the Founding Director of Kashkul and Slemani's UNESCO City of Literature. She is a 2022 NEA Fellow, the first ever working from the Kurdish.